IRELAND FOREVER IN HER HEART

Kate Morrisey Kraft

Always dream big & believe!
Kate Morrisey Kraft

COPYRIGHT © 2019 KATHLEEN MORRISEY KRAFT
All rights reserved.

ISBN: 9781698853277

DEDICATION

This book is dedicated to the memory of my late Grandmother, Catherine Charlton Conlon. She played such an integral part in my life, and I always looked upon her as my second Mom.

'Nanny' loved to have me sit close while she told her story of being raised on the West Coast of Ireland with family and friends. Then, the tone of her narrative changed dramatically, as she began her new adventures 'across the pond' in The United States.

All her life, Katie Charlton Conlon carried her tremendous loyalty and love of Ireland deep in her heart.

I would be remiss if I did not mention Nora Scanlon and Marion McGlone Donohue on this dedication page. Together, they were the *Three Irish Musketeers*. Their friendship spanned two countries, more than eighty years, and so many wonderful adventures.

They are all gone now, but never forgotten!

Lastly, a nod to our *Clan* ... whether you spell *Charlton* like my Grandmother, or *Charleton* like her brother, James ... we are all family!

FORWARD

In order to understand the language utilized by my main characters, I feel obligated to share a quick lesson in their oral quirks.

First, the Irish have the unusual habit of inventing their own contractions. For example, *dunna'* translates as '*do not.*' The same holds true for words such as *couldna'* (*could not*), '*tis* (*it is*), *tisn't* (*it isn't*), and *dinna'* (*did not*), just to name a few. Although I grew up hearing these contractions in everyday conversations, I *dinna'* want my readers to be confused!

Secondly, is the use of pronouns for emphasis. *Meself* (*myself*) is often used when referring to the first person singular. *Himself* and *herself* are often utilized after a proper name to show importance. An example of this would be the phrase, '*give the paper to John, himself.*' No one else but John is to receive the paper.

One of my favorite Irish *spoken* words is *fer-tah*. Loosely translated it means *for the purpose of.*' An example of this is the sentence, '*Mary, herself, went downstairs fer-tah do the wash.*' Why did Mary go downstairs? For the purpose of doing the wash, of course! (I find myself using this silly word all the time; however, my husband always catches it and teases me!)

Lastly, and most important, is the difficulty that the Irish have with the two consonants, **th**, at the beginning of a word. In the Gaelic language, there is no such sound at the beginning of any of their words. We always teased my Grandmother mercilessly as we forced her to say words like *think* (*tink*), *thunder* (*tunder*), and *throwback* (*trowback*).

Simple **th** words such as *they* and *there*, were pronounced as if they began with the single letter '*t*' or the letter '*d*' as the first letter of the word. An excellent example of this is our word *the*, which would be pronounced '*tah*.'

Also, at the end of each chapter you will find a shamrock ☘. The material following this sign will either be a historical explanation or an elaboration on a particular character from that particular chapter.

CHAPTER ONE

On the west coast of Ireland, north of the usual tourist attractions such as Galway Bay, Lakes of Killarney and Cliffs of Mohr, is County Sligo.

Located on the Atlantic side of the Island, it possesses a rugged yet magnificent countryside. From the air, the handcrafted stone walls that surround each property form a picture of unimaginable shades of green.

Our story begins in , Kilmacowen Parish, County Sligo. We are traveling back in time to the year 1889. A thatched roof cottage is located in the shadow of the hauntingly beautiful Ben Bulben Mountain, and the house borders on the lush forest that is only steps from the door. This is the home of the Charlton family. Anne and John, plus all six of their children live in this one-bedroom lofted cottage.

John, the father or Da, is a fisherman. This is a harsh and demanding life, but most of all it is extremely dangerous. His small wooden boat, a curragh, is not meant to traverse the stormy, unpredictable ocean. Yet, John must navigate these treacherous waters six mornings a week in order to support his family.

Anne, his wife, is very frail and has always had difficulty breathing in the damp climate of the West Coast. She relies heavily on her grown children to perform all the daily household tasks. The siblings also attend to the garden, care for the chickens, milk Millie their cow, and manage the horses. Nevertheless, they are a lively and happy family, and there never seems to be a dull moment in their household.

The Charlton cottage is continuously filled with laughter, music, song and prayer. Their strong religious beliefs are a major part of their daily lives, and keep them focused on how thankful they are to have survived English rule, the Great Potato Famine, and the widespread poverty that plagues their side of the Island. Additionally, they are always aware of how fortunate they are to have a roof over their heads and food on their table. This family never forgets to thank God daily for these gifts.

Today, however, the house is silent. Eliza, the oldest of the children, has four of her five siblings on their knees praying for their Mum who is about to give birth.

"*Dear God,*" Eliza prayed. "*Please help Mum to deliver a healthy baby. We all promise You that we will help to take care of the wee one. We ask that You please restore Mum's health after her difficult pregnancy.*"

"*Amen!*" The children answered in unison.

Hours later, as they all began to nod off to sleep, they quickly sat upright when they heard their parent's bedroom door open. Their father appeared carrying a small bundle wrapped in a soft knitted shawl.

"Da," James, his second son called out. "Is Mum alright? And are you carrying a boy or a girl babe?"

John smiled as he gazed around the room at his children's eager faces. He looked down and gently uncovered the tiny newborn. "She is a wee colleen and has entered our world just a little too early, so she is very delicate. We must all work to make sure she stays warm and healthy. Eliza," John addressed his daughter, "will you please boil some of our well water and then let it cool so she can drink."

Eliza jumped up and began to fill the kettle using the convenient kitchen water pump. Her Dad had installed the pump – considered a modern convenience – in order to make life a little easier for his pregnant wife. The past eight months had been extremely difficult for Anne, and the baby's delivery had sapped whatever strength she retained in her delicate body.

"Let us all say a silent prayer for your Mum," John proposed. "Let us ask God, our heavenly Father, to restore her health and watch over our newborn babe."

The children quickly dropped to their knees and bowed their heads. Mary, who had been the baby of the family for many years, was the first to raise her eyes. She observed tears on her Dad's cheeks and saw the deep sadness in his eyes. At that moment, Mary knew that their Mum would never be the same again. She slowly lowered her head and continued to pray with her family.

After several minutes, their father stood, handed the baby to Eliza, and then spoke to all his children. "Our baby is to be named Catherine. Mum says 'tis too long a name for such a wee colleen, so she asks we call her Katie."

Eliza lovingly gazed down at her baby sister. "Well, Katie me darlin', I suppose 'tis time we cleaned you up, put your bare bottom into a nappy, and dress you in some warm swaddling clothes. When your boiled water is cooled, we will give yourself a fine drink before Mum sees you again.

James stretched out his arms to take the baby from Eliza. "Sure, I will hold Katie while you make up her bottle. We all just want a wee bit of time with our tiny one. It is not every day we get to welcome a sister into our lives."

Mary stuck out her lower lip and pouted. "James, dunna' you remember when meself was born?"

"I just remember all the crying," James teased his younger sister. "When you were born, Mary, most of us were wee ones, and we couldna' even take care of ourselves. Now, we are all old enough to take care of Katie. Mary, even you can change her nappies. And all of us together can show her how much we love her and welcome her with open arms into our family."

Suddenly, James stopped speaking and intensely studied the tiny face of the infant that he held in his arms. He looked up at his Dad with a puzzled expression and deep concern reflected in his eyes.

"Da, why does Katie's skin have a slight olive tinge to it? Is she sick, Da? Please tell us!"

John gave a hearty laugh. "Oh me Jimmie, our Katie is a *trowback*."

James appeared very disturbed when his father used the word *throwback*.

"No! You canna' *trow* her back, Da! God would surely condemn you to everlasting hell for such a ting!"

John used his hand to cover his laughter. "No son, *trowback* is not as bad as it sounds. Instead, it refers to an event in history, hundreds of years ago, when English ships defeated tah Spanish Armada right here, off our very coast of Sligo."

"What's an armada?" Willy asked.

"Well, good question me boy! An armada 'tis a collection of ships which are equipped with cannons and ready to go to war at any time. Spain's Armada was strongest in our world, until England attacked and defeated it. Your Great-Great Grandfather wrote down in his journal about tah terrible battle. He watched from a high point on our very own land. And when all fighting was done, he kissed his wife farewell and took his boat, his currach, out to sea to rescue sailors. Our whole town showed up to save men, as well as cargo, from the destroyed ships. Even pieces of wood floating on water were dragged ashore to be used again. Nothing was left to be seen!

James was intrigued. "I never knew your Great-Granda's story, but I am still very confused about how Spain's defeat can have anything to do with our precious Katie?"

"James," his Dad continued, "now comes tah most important part of me story. Spanish sailors fell in love with County Sligo and decided not to return to Spain. Eventually, sailors married our local girls from town and had children. Sometimes, newborns had very dark hair, brown eyes, and olive skin tones. People started calling tah babes '*dark Irish*.' As the years went by, and more and more women intermarried, decedents had less and less of the sailors' traits. But, every once in a while, some characteristics would unexpectantly pop up ... *trowbacks*!"

"I canna' tell you how much better I feel, Da! Your story helps to explain your word, *trowback*. I really believed our little Katie might be seriously ill and turning yellow!"

"My dear son, you know in your heart we will love Katie no matter if her eyes are brown, her hair dark, or her skin slightly olive. All of you are treasured gifts from God, and Mum and I love all of you!"

"Do you hear your Da, little Katie?" Michael asked. "We are going to treasure you forever and ever."

Then, all the children gathered around their new sister, counting her fingers and toes, looking closely at the color of her hair, and trying to assess the flecks of color in her eyes.

"Now, Katie does seem to have one problem." Their Dad explained. "Since she was born very early, she does not weigh much and her lungs do not seem to be fully developed. Mum is afraid Katie will have difficulty taking breaths, so we have to help her by using steam from boiling pots of water to make sure we keep her airways open. 'Tis a lot of extra work for all of us."

Eliza's eyes filled with tears as she sent a quiet prayer heavenward. *"Please, dear Lord, watch over our little Katie. Bless us with all knowledge to know how to take care of her. Amen.*

Suddenly, Eliza was jarred from her own thoughts, when she heard her father speak again. "Willy, me son, will you please run to O'Neill's house and ask Misses, herself, if we could buy some goat's milk for Katie?"

Willy frowned. "I dunna understand, Da. Why would we need goat milk when we have Millie, our own cow, right outside in our barn?"

John was very patient with his son as he explained his reasons. "Since Katie is what Doctor Keighron calls premature, her stomach will be very delicate and sensitive. Mum is a little too weak to nurse her, so we need to feed her a milk a little easier to digest. Now, run along, me son!"

Quick as a flash, Willy was out the door and running down the dirt roadway.

John turned his attention to his oldest daughter. "Eliza, when Willy returns with milk, could you please bring it to a gentle boil, cool it, and make us some bottles? Will you and James please place all filled bottles outside in our cooling cellar to be safe? I know 'tis very late, but we must teach Katie to latch on to her bottle in order to feed."

Eliza hugged her father. "Sure, Da, we are happy to help anyway we can. James and meself will even unpack all our baby clothes, and we will make certain we have enough soft nappies cut to last for several days before we have to wash her used ones."

John wiped a tear from his eye with his shirtsleeve. "I dunna know what we would ever do without all of you to help. *God bless each and every one of you, and always keep you safe in the palm of His hand!*"

    Life was difficult for the Charlton Clan. They relied heavily on their faith to see them through harsh English rule, famine, plague, and rough seas.

    The soil in Sligo was rocky and very poor quality, only fit for potato crops and some hardy vegetables. Therefore, the men were forced to look to the Atlantic Ocean and fishing for their survival. Each morning, the fishermen ventured out on unpredictable seas in their small wooden boats, or curraghs. Many never returned from their dangerous expeditions … forever lost in a watery grave. Those that did return, were forced to sell their catch in the town marketplace to the British overseers at extremely low prices.

    In 1588, the English navy defeated the Spanish Armada off the coast of Sligo. England now emerged as the most powerful nation in the world, and immediately began plans to protect themselves from any future enemy seeking to over-throw their world domination. Ireland, with only a small strip of water separating it from England, offered the greatest advantage as a staging area to attack the new world power.

    In the 1600's, English Parliament authorized Oliver Cromwell to invade Ireland

and conquer its inhabitants. Their ultimate goal was to take control of all the Irish port cities; thus, preventing their enemies from using its close proximity to attack England. Parliament granted full power to Cromwell, and commissioned his army to take any action necessary to achieve this end.

Unfortunately, Oliver Cromwell believed in the 'take no prisoners' rule of battle. He ordered his forces to kill, destroy all crops, and burn the land as they marched through the Emerald Isle. Cromwell issued specific instructions to cleanse the land of all Irish Catholics and instill fear in the hearts of all inhabitants; thus, establishing his reign of terror.

On the east coast of Ireland, north of the capital city of Dublin, there is a fertile area called the Boyne River Valley. The town of Drogheda (drow-hee-dra) is located along the scenic banks of the river. In the 17th century, the inhabitants of this valley were peaceful farmers. However, when Cromwell arrived, he decided to teach the Catholic a lesson in his ultimate power. He commissioned his army to kill all men, women, and children in the valley; then, burn the land to the ground. After this senseless slaughter, Parliament unsuccessfully tried to reign in Cromwell's desire to eliminate all Irish Catholics.

The English army marched south from Dublin, through Wexford, Waterford, Cork and Kerry. Then the forces traveled up the west coast all the way to Donegal, as they captured every port city.

Historically, Cromwell's hatred toward the Irish Catholic is very well documented. He continued to execute Catholic priests and bishops without a trial, and then burned their monasteries to the ground. The homes and lands of any Catholic were seized and reassigned to all individuals loyal to the British Crown. Parliament also awarded Irish land grants to any Englishman who donated funds directly to the Irish campaign. Ultimately, more than 60% of Ireland's land was given away to English loyalists.

Thus, began England's harsh rule over the Irish.

CHAPTER TWO

Katie's early childhood was plagued by sickness. Since she was a premature birth, her lungs were not fully developed and she continuously suffered from bronchial infections and very high fevers.

Moreover, Anne, her Mum, was still confined to bed, never regaining her strength after Katie's birth. Tearfully, Anne listened from her bedroom as her baby daughter struggled for every breath.

Eliza, however, never left her sister's side. Day and night, she struggled with heavy pots of boiling water in order to produce the steam to ease Katie's breathing.

One difficult night in particular, James observed Eliza's fatigue and the dark circles under her eyes.

"Please, Eliza, let me sit tonight with Katie. I would be pleased to carry hot pots and set up her blanket tent to capture steam. You need to take care of yourself, Eliza, so you are strong enough to take care of Katie."

"James, I canna' leave her alone, and I would never be able to rest from my worry. She is like me own wee child!"

James thought for a moment while he tried to rationalize Eliza's strong bond with the newborn. "Well," he proposed, "what if I read to Katie while you rest in Mum's rocking chair. I will carry all replacement pots and tend to our fire."

Eliza smiled and handed James the family Bible, the only bound book that was owned by the Charlton family. "I have been reading from Book of Psalms, James. I dunna know if she understands God's words, but my voice seems to relax her and she seems to struggle less with each breath."

James began to read aloud with a calm and relaxing lilt in his voice. Soon, Eliza found herself drifting off to sleep with her evening prayers still on her lips. James smiled and continued to read, pleased that he was able to help both his sisters at one time.

Suddenly, Eliza awoke with a start. When she looked up and wiped the sleep from her eyes, she saw her brother walking the floor with Katie in his arms while he sang some of his favorite lullabies to the contented baby.

"Oh, James," Eliza whispered, "wee Katie is smiling up at you with such love in her eyes!"

James laughed. "I really doubt she is smiling, me darlin', 'tis just gas since Katie just finished her bottle."

"Surely I know a difference 'tween a smile and some gas." Eliza argued. "Katie is watching you and following you with her big brown cow eyes!"

"Sure, 'tis strange to look in Katie's eyes and not see our same blue color each of us have. I believe she is 'tis tah only person I know who has deep brown eyes with flecks of gold." James observed. "Unusual, but truly beautiful."

"Perhaps one day we can go to our old schoolhouse and find a picture of a Spanish royal in a history book." Eliza suggested. "I believe Katie would resemble a member of Spanish nobility. Just stand back and observe her perfect nose, her perfect angel lips, and beautiful brown eyes. She must have royal blood!"

Once again, James laughed at his sister's observations. Their Uncle Michael was always trying to convince the family that the Charlton's descended from a royal house in England. He claimed that back in the early 1600's they were awarded an Irish land grant due to their loyalty to the Crown. James smiled as he recalled the conversation. He wondered if they would ever learn the truth of their family history.

At that moment, their Dad entered the cottage and laughed heartily at his two grown children. "Have you both been into me potato moonshine? All your talk about royalty and nobility – tell me, where are our jewels and show me our pot of gold! Where are our servants cooking dinner or working out in our fields completing spring planting?"

Oh, Da!" Eliza continued with their game. "Sure gold 'tis somewhere on our land. Perhaps hidden in one of our outbuildings or buried deep along our creek bed."

"Eliza, me darlin', it would just be easier for us to follow a rainbow and search for a leprechaun's pot of gold!"

James thought for a moment. "Da, do you really believe all our stories about Ireland's leprechauns? Surely, you must have seen one yourself during your younger years?"

"And who is to say I am not still in me younger years?" John joked with his son. "Perhaps tonight, after we sup, will be a perfect time to tell a tale or two about our famous leprechauns."

Both Eliza and James were thrilled. They loved to sit by the turf fire and listen to the tales that had been passed down from generation to generation.

During this period in Irish history, most of the Catholic school-aged children only attended classes until the sixth-grade level. English students, however, always attended a different school through the secondary level. Then, they would make the decision to continue their higher education in Dublin, or return to England to attend University.

By the time a west coast child reached the sixth grade, their reading skills were fairly well established, as well as their ability to perform simple mathematics. On the coast, their teachers were lenient with the students who missed classes during the potato planting and harvesting seasons. They referred to these days as '*potato holidays.*'

In 1592, Queen Elizabeth I established Trinity College in Dublin. Catholics were barred from the College until 1793. However, in 1854, The University College of Dublin was established. Although known as 'Catholic University,' it admitted all religions.

Practically every Irish home contained a Bible, and this is where the children honed their reading skills. It was not uncommon for a detailed family history to be recorded in the first pages of the Bible. Then, the Bible would be handed down from generation to generation.

The name *Charlton* can be traced back to a royal house in England. It was believed that during the 1500's they were awarded an Irish land grant as a reward for their service to the crown. History does show that the family lost favor with England sometime in the late 1600's. This would have been the time that the Charlton's converted from the Church of England to Catholicism. However, they continued to live in Sligo, and maintained ownership of the family homestead and the surrounding lands.

The fact that the Charlton family lived within walking distance of the port of Sligo, was another example of respect for their one-time loyalty to the Crown. English penal law prohibited any Irish Catholic from living within a five-mile radius of any port city.

Turf or *peat*, that is still burned today in Irish fireplaces, is an organic fuel that is literally cut in brick-sized blocks from a bog. It is composed of the partial remains of animals and decayed vegetation. Scientists believe that turf dates back to the era of the dinosaur and has thrived in the damp, wet, and poorly drained environment of the west coast.

It should be noted that turf is the first step in the production of coal.

I know first-hand, that it is very difficult work to cut peat. A two-sided spade is utilized to slice the bricks of fuel. Then, it must be lifted from the bog and transported to the home. My Great-Uncle Paddy used a donkey and cart to haul his bricks home.

Burning peat gives off a very earthy smell. It is certainly not offensive, but totally different from our wood-burning fireplaces.

CHAPTER THREE

After supper was served and the dishes cleaned and dried, the children gathered their homemade stools around the turf fire and prepared to enjoy one of their father's wonderful tales.

Before James and Eliza settled down for the evening, they waited patiently outside their parent's bedroom door in order to help support their Mum to her favorite rocking chair.

Totally surprised, the younger children jumped up and gathered around their Mum ... hugging, kissing, and laughing ... so thrilled to have their family together for the evening. Katie, however, was unaware of all the excitement as she slept peacefully in her warm basket next to the fireplace.

As everyone settled down, James turned to his father. "Da, I do believe tonight's story is to be about our little people."

"Yes, me boy, our famous Irish leprechaun is our story tonight. Let me begin at his early history. A leprechaun is considered just one of many fairies livin' in Ireland. He is not very tall, maybe two feet, and appears to be quite old with his long white beard. But never be fooled because our wee fairy is as fast as a young jackrabbit! A leprechaun is extremely clever and incredibly smart too. Indeed, it is said he can trick his way out of captivity almost every time someone manages to trap him."

"I am sorry to interrupt," Willy apologized, "but what about a girl leprechaun?"

"Oh Willy, you always ask such good questions!" His father exclaimed. "Nowhere in history is anything written about a female leprechaun. We have many other women fairies on our island, just not a lady leprechaun."

James chuckled. "'Tis no wonder why! A wee fairy man lives on his own and works under protection of darkness late into tah night. He has no wife to demand he be home to supper, and no one to spend his hard-earned gold. Sure, he can come and go as free as a bird with no responsibilities!"

Everyone laughed at James' bit of humor. They quieted down as soon as their Mum spoke, directing her comments to her older son. "Living alone with no one to keep him company may be one reason why a leprechaun gets himself into so much mischief. No wife and no children to come home to is not a romantic idea, my dear James. It can be a very lonely life." Then, Anne turned to her husband with a twinkle in her eye. "Please continue with your story, me love."

John smiled at his beloved wife and settled back to continue his tale. "It has mostly been forgotten, but actually we have two types of leprechauns ... our green one is a cobbler and works hard making shoes for all our other fairies. He takes his money and hides it in a kettle usually deep within a forest. You see, my children, all our fairies love to dance and quickly wear out shoes. Immediately, the green leprechaun gets to work making a new pair and is happy to take gold for his efforts and add it to his hidden stash.

But beware of our red leprechaun! He is mischievous and sometimes a hurtful fairy! If you find everything in your house turned upside down, or on a cold night your fire has been doused, it is our red leprechaun at work. He snatches freshly baked pies from cooling ledges, and both pie and its tin are never seen again. On a quiet night you can hear him laugh as he opens up paddock gates and lets tah animals loose. Unlike his green cousin who likes to move around and travel our countryside, a red leprechaun tends to live in just one home and continually torment and trick its residents!"

Mary looked very troubled. "A red fairy is not very nice if being bad is his only job! Da, I would love to have a green leprechaun come and live with us. He could make us shoes whenever we needed a new pair. Maybe we could even be fortunate enough to have two pairs of shoes!"

"Well," John began, "I tink we will talk about our green leprechaun tonight. Me own Mum told me about a neighbor in Tobercurry, just down our road a piece, and how Mrs. Fahey's son actually held a leprechaun in his own hands."

"Oh!" Whispered the children, totally in awe. They had never heard this particular tale before tonight.

Instantly, John knew that he had captured the full attention of his offspring. He smiled as he viewed their anxious faces.

"We already know if you catch a leprechaun, he must either give you his pot of gold or else grant you wishes. You must tell him which one you want before he has a chance to escape.

"I would take all my wishes at one time." James proudly announced.

Eliza scowled. "Oh no, James! Take his pot of gold at once and be on your way a very rich man!"

Mary and Willy sat silently and never uttered a word. Their faces reflected the fact that they were anxiously awaiting the continuation of their father's story.

"Well," John began again. "Everyone knew Seumas Fahey was an extremely lazy lad. He never did his chores in early morning like all his neighbors. Instead, he would laze around all day doing whatever he felt like doing. As late afternoon approached, his Mum would threaten him with no supper unless he completed all his chores. Seumas loved to eat, so he would finally get himself to moving. He fed his chickens, milked his cow, and finally looked over at all tah weeds flourishing in his Mum's garden. He would tell himself der weeds would still be growing tomorrow, and bypass his chore completely. With only one more task left on his list, Seumas just had to check on his old mare, Peg, and make sure she had food and water. After taking care of Peg, it was off to the kitchen for a nice warm supper. As Seumas approached his barn, he heard a tap-tap-tapping, followed by whistling – a most beautiful sound to behold. It appeared to be coming from his mare's stall; however, where he stood, distance made it impossible to see anyone. As Seumas crept closer, he finally saw a little old man partially hidden in shadow, busy making a pair of shoes. Due to all his tapping and whistling, he never heard Seumas approach."

"Oh, no! Run, little man ... run!" Michael shouted as his Dad took a wee sip from his moonshine cup.

"It is no use to call out, Michael!" John advised his son. "Seumas reached out and captured his leprechaun before he even knew what had happened. "Give me your gold or grant my wishes, Mr. Leprechaun!" Seumas demanded from the little old man.

"I will gladly give you all me gold if you but loosen your hold on me. For I canna' breathe in your tight fist! I promise to give you whatever you want, but if I am departed from life, you will never know me secret to me hidden treasure!"

"Well," John continued, "Seumas dinna' know once you have a firm grip on a leprechaun, you must never loosen your hold. But Seumas felt sorry for tah old man and opened his hand. Quick as a wink, his leprechaun jumped down and created a small cloud of dust. Seumas looked away in order to protect his eyes; however, when he turned back, his leprechaun had tricked him, and was nowhere to be found. Seumas learned a hard lesson ... never, never take your eyes off your captured fairy.

"Hooray!" Shouted Michael and Mary in unison.

Their Dad laughed. "So me dear children, you are cheering for Mr. Leprechaun's artful escape? Well tink of poor Seumas' feelings. He was so distraught over his loss of money and wishes, he just wandered aimlessly around his horse's stall. Without looking where he was going, Seumas suddenly tripped over some unseen object and fell down very hard on his hands and knees. When he opened his eyes, he was looking directly at a tiny work bench with a beautiful pair of petite shoes encrusted with precious gemstones. He picked up tah diminutive shoes and gently put both in his jacket's padded pocket. Quickly, he headed off at a run to his Mum's kitchen. When Seumas arrived, he was out of breath, his face was very red, and his words didn't seem to make any sense to his Mum. She led her son to a chair and carefully helped him to sit. Mrs. Fahey was very worried he might have hurt his head while he was outside completing his chores. Imagine her surprise, when Seumas pulled miniature shoes out of his pocket and gingerly placed both on her kitchen table."

"Oh!" Whispered John's children, completely mesmerized by his story.

"Now, Mrs. Fahey was spellbound by her son's discovery. When she had a moment to recover, she knew tah precious little shoes could be used to prove to everyone leprechauns existed!

"Are Fahey's rich after Seumas' discovery?" James asked.

"Not right away," his Dad replied. "Mrs. Fahey was a very shrewd woman, so she ordered her son to build a locked glass box to protect his treasure. Now, it would cost visitors a few pennies to stare into his box. People came from all around the country. By mule or horseback, and some visitors walked long distances to see his leprechaun's stunning shoes. Mrs. Fahey sold drinks along with scones and cookies to all weary travelers, generating even more income for her family.

"Did you or Mum ever get to see Seumas' wee shoes?" Eliza asked.

"We both did!" Her Mum replied in a soft voice. "We saw his leprechaun's wee shoes before both were locked in Seumas' glass box. I actually held both shoes in one hand – so beautiful and so very tiny- it was truly a day to remember! I always hoped a wee bit of magic from his shoes would rub off on me hands. And indeed, it did! I married your father and I was blessed with each one of you!"

John could visibly see how exhausted Anne had become from the exertion of sitting up in a chair all evening. "Now, me dears," he addressed his children, "it is time for all of us to say goodnight until tomorrow. Before we part, let me tell you one more fact about our legendary leprechaun. It has been told for hundreds of years, if you follow a rainbow you will find a pot of gold at its end. I dunna' know how many people have ever been successful, but always keep that dream alive in your heart. Now, kisses and hugs all around, me loves, and off to your loft and your evening prayers."

After the children had settled down in the sleeping loft, John picked up his wife and carried her to their bedroom. John's heart broke as he realized how light and fragile Anne felt in his arms. In the short walk to the bed, she had already tucked her head against his chest and was sound asleep. John carefully laid Anne down on the bed with his arms still tightly wrapped around her. He prayed all night that God would give him the strength to survive Anne's declining health.

The leprechaun is a tale of an Irish fairy that is still told in Ireland today. It is believed that they are the descendants of ancient royalty and have been blessed with long lives – more than two hundred years. They are also very talented musicians on the fiddle, tin whistle, and the Irish harp.

Another popular instrument is the bodhran. Although its origin is disputed, it has been recorded that it was first made from the animal skins that were utilized to haul the fresh cut peat from the bog. It was stretched tight over willow branches so that it resembled a drum. It was struck by a tiny wooden hammer that was attached by a cord. The 'poor man's' bodhran had pennies attached so that when the drum was struck, the pennies added the sound of a tambourine to the instrument.

The leprechaun's greatest joy has always been to dance to the fairy music and perform all the traditional jigs and reels. Therefore, they would wear out their shoes very quickly and turn to the green leprechaun to make a new pair.

If you are fortunate enough to catch a leprechaun, either by following a rainbow or listening for his tap-tap of his cobbler's hammer, never loosen your grip on him, and never, ever lose eye contact. If you do, he will be gone in the blink of an eye, and so too will be your three wishes and his pot of gold.

Sligo's famous author and poet, William Butler Yeats, wrote a collection of stories entitled *Irish Fairies*. Although still in print, it is best to look for copies in used book stores.

CHAPTER FOUR

"Katie, bring yourself into tah kitchen fer your supper!" Eliza called out the window to her eight-year-old sister.

The youngest sibling laughed out loud when she heard her sister's summons. Katie wondered if Eliza was aware that her Irish brogue dramatically thickened whenever she raised her voice.

"Sure, I am coming right away!" Katie responded as she ran toward the house, her dark auburn curls bounced as she galloped on her stick horse through the front door.

The thatched roof cottage was warm and welcoming, no easy task with the cold damp climate of winter in County Sligo. Eliza also worked hard to ensure that her family was always well fed, their clothes clean and mended, and the house in perfect order. Being the oldest of seven children, Eliza believed that her role in life was to serve as both the mother and sister to their large family. Her Mum, still sickly, was confined to her bed, while her Dad left the house before sunrise to fish on the early morning sea in order to secure a good catch. Then, her Dad would spend the remainder of the day in the town square selling his fish to the wealthy

English inhabitants. His children never ceased to worry until their father was back on dry land, with his currach tied safely to the dock. They always paused during their morning chores to send a quick prayer heavenward asking for their Dad's safe return from the unpredictable seas.

"Is Da home yet?" Katie called as she continued to gallop around the room.

"No, not yet, me darlin'. Our market tisn't closed yet, and you know how Da always stays a little later just in case someone still needs some of his fish." Eliza explained. "Now, ride your stick horse outside to our pump and wash your face and hands. Make sure you come directly to table, Katie, with no more distractions!"

"Come on horsey, let's go fast!" Katie giggled as she pranced outside to the pump. "My horse is a grand old fellow!" She called over her shoulder. "I tink we are old enough to ride by ourselves over to Dublin for its famous horse show!"

James and Michael laughed at their sister's shenanigans. Eliza gave both her brothers a very stern look. "Dunna' encourage Katie, boyos! She has to learn Dublin is just too far away and cost of a horseshow way too dear for our pockets."

"Oh, Eliza," James interrupted, "let her have her harmless fun. Sure, Katie has been sickly all winter and deserves to have some dreams of adventure."

"Katie needs to have a clear vision of what reality is like on our west coast!" Eliza scolded her brother. "Ever since we suffered through the Great Potato Famine, we have all learned our dreams hardly ever come true. Katie needs to leave her imagination behind with her childhood, and face what her life will be like as she grows. Just like all her friends, she will eventually marry a local farmer, have babies, and settle down to help run a farm."

Katie galloped back inside the house and took her seat at the small wooden table. "Did I hear you speak of me goin' to our Dublin horse show? Can we travel all across our country just to see beautiful show horses?"

Katie's eyes were sparkling and her whole face glowed with happiness. Eliza was forever taken aback by her sister's striking features. Of the seven children, Katie was the only one who exhibited traits of a Spanish ancestor.

Eliza's voice softened as she turned and spoke directly to her sister. "My sweet one," Eliza began, "Aunt Bea and Uncle Peter sent word Pandora, Uncle Peter's favorite horse, has given birth to a handsome foal. He is anxious to show him off to our family and has asked us to come for an afternoon visit. How do you feel about making our trip tomorrow?"

Katie jumped up and down, clapping her hands enthusiastically. "Oh yes, dear Eliza! Going to Aunt Bea and Uncle Peter's farm is just as good as going to a horse show!" She hugged her sister tightly around the waist. "I love you so, so much for your kind plans!"

Suddenly, Katie stopped her celebration, sat down on the floor, and appeared as if she might break down and cry. "Who will be here to take care of our Mum? We canna' go to Uncle Peter's barn with no one home to take care of herself!"

"Dunna' worry about it, angel." James comforted his sister. "Michael and meself will take care of Mum so you will be able to go with Eliza and enjoy a special day with no worries or concerns!"

"I love you too, James!" Katie declared as she wrapped her arms around her brother. "Promise me you will never go away and leave me. I dunna know what I would ever do if you were not here with me!"

James looked deeply saddened as he averted direct eye contact while he promised to always stay with Katie. It was a fact that soon James would be asked by his father to leave his homeland and travel abroad in search of employment. This would enable James to send money home to help support his family back in Ireland. His oldest brother, John, had already emigrated to Germany in search of employment.

The following morning, Katie was up with the sun and ready for her daily chores in the garden and in the barn. She said her morning prayers as she cleaned the barn stalls and collected eggs. Then, Katie was off to the garden to pull any weeds that had infiltrated the ground around their precious plants. Finally, she was off to milk their one cow, Millie. The Charlton family knew how fortunate they were to have milk in their diet. They had learned from the handwritten journal of their Grandfather, how they survived the potato famine by stealing milk from the British over-seer.

Having completed all her chores, Katie entered the house in search of Eliza. "Are you ready for our ride, dear sister?" Katie asked as she washed her hands at the kitchen water pump.

Once again, Eliza scowled at her sister. "Katie! You should not wash up at the kitchen pump. We use it only for cooking and dishes, not dirty hands with mud caked under your fingernails! Now, outside with you until you are clean!"

"But Eliza," Katie tried to justify her actions, "I was in such a hurry to finish my chores so we could go to see Uncle Peter's newborn foal. And our indoor kitchen pump is the fastest and the warmest way to get clean!"

"James," Eliza addressed her brother, "please tell your sister the rules of our home. And also refresh her memory; we do not stand up and eat our breakfast. We sit and eat at our kitchen table with clean hands!"

"Do not look to me to correct our little sister." James warned Eliza. "I will not try to take a strong wind out of her sails of life! She is so full of energy and happy to complete her morning chores. So, let us be thankful for her cheerful personality! Rest assured, I will never become her bossy older brother!"

Eliza just shook her head and walked away from the table. She realized that James did not want to have any part in Katie's discipline. He was her friend, the one person she could rely upon and tell her deepest secrets. Actually, Eliza was happy that James had assumed this role. Their Mum was still confined to bed, and their absentee father was busy working long hours. Katie desperately needed a father-figure in her life, and James was perfect for the role.

James sat back and watched as Eliza hitched their work horse to the buggy. He wanted to step forward and help, but he respected Eliza's strong feelings of independence, as well as her need to prove herself capable of all the farm tasks. James silently stood on the threshold of the cottage until the horse and buggy were harnessed for their trip. Then, he quietly advanced and lifted Katie up on to the seat of the wagon.

"Now, me darlins'," James advised, "be careful with all deep road ruts since it will be very easy to break a wheel. Just steer into them and have a good ride to Aunt Beatrice's."

Eliza smiled down at her over-protective brother, while Katie bounced up and down on the buckboard seat anxious to begin a new adventure.

"Goodbye, sweet James!" Katie called over her shoulder as the buggy pulled away. "I love you!"

The Dublin Horse Show is a very famous event throughout Great Britain, Europe, and Asia. Held in Ballsbridge, just outside of Dublin proper, competitors come great distances to participate in this annual event.

The show, begun in 1864, has even included members of England's royal family. Although horses were first awarded prizes for their lineage and beauty as they were walked around the show ring by their handlers, now, the horse show is strictly a jumping competition.

During Eliza's explanation regarding why Katie could not attend the horse show, she uses the word *dear*. While in Ireland, I found myself totally confused about the many definitions of this word. Finally, it was explained that one of its meanings is *expensive*. Therefore, when a salesclerk in Dublin told me that the sweater I was considering was 'very dear,' she actually meant that the cost was very high.

Beatrice (Bea) and Peter Harrison were Katie's biological aunt and uncle. Bea was John Charlton's sister, and together with her husband, Peter, they owned a family farm not far from the Charlton's original homestead.

Ireland's potato famine, also known as *The Great Hunger*, occurred between 1845 and 1852. At this time, Ireland was still governed by England under the title of *The United Kingdom of Great Britain and Ireland*.

Prior to the potato famine, the British Parliament had passed harsh laws against the Irish Catholic. These penal laws prohibited all Catholics from owning or leasing land in their own country. They were denied the right to vote, and could not hold any political office. Catholics were deprived of an education and prohibited by law from becoming professionals. The final law, prevented any Irish Catholic from living within a five-mile radius of any port city.

The Catholic population was forced to live in ghettos and worked for British landlords. In return, they were given a small patch of land and warned that the only crop they could grow was the potato. Ultimately, the potato became the sole food for the poor. It is estimated that the average Irish family consumed approximately seven pounds of potatoes per day. Meanwhile, on the European continent, potatoes were viewed as a delicious secondary dish to their meat. Therefore, most of the potato harvest was exported and profited the British landlord.

In 1845, a potato blight began to destroy the leaves and tubers of the plant. Approximately 1.5 million of the poor died of starvation. Concurrently, a cholera epidemic developed, adding to the misery and the death toll. More than a million of the starving Irish Catholics were forced to emigrate to The United States in order to survive.

In 1879, a second potato blight occurred. There was widespread panic; however, the Irish that were now living in The United States, banded together and contributed millions of dollars and tons of food to the starving in their home country. A new railroad system had been built in order to connect the capital city of Dublin with the major cities on the west coast. The railroad was able to deliver food and supplies to the starving inhabitants.

The famine brought about two major changes within the Catholic communities. The first was the formation of pockets of resistance that were willing to fight and die for basic freedoms, and, eventually total independence from the Crown.

The second was the resurgence of the Catholic religion throughout the Isle. In 1879, the Blessed Virgin, Saint Joseph, and Saint John the Evangelist appeared on the south gable of the Church at Knock.

Fifteen witnesses all testified in exact detail what they all saw at the church on an August evening. Although it was pouring rain, the area around the apparition remained completely dry for more than two hours. The Vatican embraced the Marian Apparition at the Knock Shrine. Word of the miracle quickly spread across Ireland and the Catholics rejoiced and had faith that they were saved. The threat of famine ended, and the plague was contained. However, the Irish had a long fight ahead of them for independence.

CHAPTER FIVE

♥

Eliza and Katie totally enjoyed their day at their Aunt and Uncle's farm. Uncle Peter walked them down to the barn to visit Pandora, and he was anxious for them to meet her new foal.

Katie laughed at the baby's shaky legs as he stood to nurse. "Just look at his long skinny legs," Katie giggled. "Not even as big around as our old boom stick!"

Eliza smiled at her sister's analogy. "This foal is only two days old, me darlin'. You dinna' even stand and walk until you were almost one year old!"

"But look at me now, Eliza! I can run and jump and skip and hop and …"

"Hold on now, Katie, and take a breath!" Eliza cautioned. "You always get so excited about any new adventure and you forget to breathe!"

Uncle Peter stood back and watched the two sisters interact. He totally enjoyed their company and all their enthusiasm over the little things that life had to offer them.

"Katie, me sweet, would you like to name our wee pony yourself?" Uncle Peter asked the rambunctious child. "Surely, it would save Aunt Bea and meself from trying to concoct a clever name for our wee boy."

Katie stopped dead in her tracks and looked up at her uncle in complete surprise. "Are you sure Uncle Peter? Maybe Eliza and meself can put our heads together and find the perfect name for Pandora's baby! Is my idea alright with you, Uncle?"

"I believe it is a perfect plan, Katie. Both Eliza and yourself can put your pretty heads together and agree on an appropriate choice for a name."

Katie stood on her toes, wrapped her arms around her Uncle's neck, and lovingly kissed his cheek. Then, without any fear, she climbed the highest rail of the fence and kissed Pandora and the foal on their noses. "I will see you both tomorrow, me dears, and we will have a special naming ceremony for your handsome new baby!"

The three of them slowly walked back to the horse and cart, waving goodbye to Aunt Bea as she strung the wash on the line to dry.

Uncle Peter smiled at the girls as he waved goodbye to his happy nieces. However, he had no idea what was in store for them when they arrived home.

Once the wagon was underway, Katie found it hard to sit still and control all her pent-up enthusiasm. Eliza, however, had her eyes focused on the road, navigating the deep ruts to avoid breaking an axle or a wheel. She smiled as Katie bounced up and down on the seat and jabbered on about their day.

"Oh, Eliza, we must discover a most perfect name for Pandora's baby. Maybe we can come up with a boy's name rhyming with Pandora. Eliza, can you think of any rhyming words?"

Eliza never took her eyes off the road as she thought of a reply to Katie's question. "Well, me sweet, Pandora seems to be a very complicated name to find a rhyming word to go with it. Maybe we should look at Pandora's character in mythology."

"What is mythology?" Katie questioned.

"Well," Eliza explained, "our schoolhouse has a book about all the gods in Greek and Roman mythology. Not our one true God we believe in, me darlin'. I am talking about hundreds and hundreds of years ago, before baby Jesus was even born. People livin' on earth needed stories to explain nature's events, like tunder storms and changes of seasons. So, someone made up stories about gods having control, like puppeteers, over all happenings. All stories put together make up mythology."

Katie finally understood and smiled at her sister. "Mythology begins with myth, and I know a myth is not a fact. So, I shouldna' believe. Now Eliza, where does Pandora's name fit into your mythology?"

"Zeus," Eliza continued, "was king of the gods and lived high atop his own mountain. He was very powerful and ruled with a heavy hand. Prometheus was a lesser god, but he was a trickster and always in trouble. One day, he stole fire from Zeus and took it down to earth to mortal man. Zeus was furious with Prometheus for stealing such a valuable life-saving force, and Zeus wanted revenge! He had Prometheus chained to a tree where an eagle had her nest. An eagle is Zeus' symbol of power, so in mythology try to remember everything has a purpose. His eagle would come every day and feed on Prometheus' liver. Overnight, Zeus would regenerate his liver so his eagle could munch on it once again tah very next day."

"'Tis a terrible story, Eliza! He dinna' deserve so harsh of a punishment!"

"Oh, Katie, please remember I am just telling you made-up stories! If it makes you feel any better, in another myth Hercules saves Prometheus."

"Good for Hercules!" Katie cried. "Now, what about Pandora? How does she fit into mythology?"

"Well," Eliza continued, "Zeus also wanted revenge on humans for using his fire. So, he called for one of his lesser gods and told him to create a woman made out of clay. Zeus named her Pandora, a name in Greek mythology meaning *all gifts*. Zeus gave Pandora a box filled with all the evils of our world, like sickness, plagues, pain, and hard work. Silly Pandora was a very curious woman, so when Zeus told her she should never open his box, Pandora became so consumed with knowing what was inside, she just had to quench her curiosity. Finally, she couldna' wait any longer, and deliberately opened Zeus' box. Pandora was horrified with all tah evil let loose on mankind. She struggled to quickly close it back up, but she was only able to save *hope*, which was trapped down in a bottom corner of Zeus' box.

"Wow!" Katie exclaimed. "Tisn't it quite a story! And, Eliza, because of your myth, I just came up with a perfect name for Pandora's baby ... Zeus! Aunt Bea and Uncle Peter's foal should be named Zeus! After all, he was responsible for creating Pandora and making her curious enough to open his box and let out all evils and disease.

At that moment, their buggy rounded the last corner in the road, and their cottage came into view. Eliza was concentrating on the road and was not able to see what Katie noticed parked at the side of their cottage.

"Hurry, Eliza!" Katie cried. "Doctor Keighron's buggy is parked at our house. Please, hurry! Mum must be in a bad way!"

In the original mythological tale of Pandora, Zeus gave her a jar to carry down from Mount Olympus to earth. History recorded that during a translation the word *jar* was inadvertently translated as *box*. This mistake was never corrected. Historians felt that the word *box* was a more appropriate word for the story.

Also. I would like to reiterate the fact that the Irish language did not use the letters **TH** at the beginning of any word. Instead, if they were faced with such a foreign word, they would pronounce any' *th'* as simply a '*t*' or a '*d*' sound.

Another strange fact about the Gaelic language is that a native speaker had no difficulty with the '*th*' at the end of a word. In this case, they pronounced it as a hard, guttural sound.

CHAPTER SIX

♥

Eliza snapped the reins against the flank of the old horse in an effort to move him more quickly. She prayed that the doctor was only paying a friendly visit to their cottage, and nothing more.

As soon as the wagon stopped, Eliza jumped down and ran to the house. Katie, on the other hand, struggled to make her way down from the high seat of the wagon. When Katie reached the opened doorway, she found her sister, Mary, sobbing while James attempted to console her.

"Is Da with Mum?" Katie asked her brother. James lifted his head and replied with one word, "No!"

Before anyone could even blink an eye, Katie was out the door and running full strength in the direction of the town marketplace. All the while, she repeated the same prayer over and over again.

"Please God, have mercy on our Mum. Dunna' take her to heaven to be with You just yet. Please, please, let her stay a little longer with us!"

When Katie arrived totally out of breath at her father's fish stand, her Dad looked up and immediately knew that his wife was in terrible danger. He quickly guided his daughter to the horse and cart while his fellow merchants watched sympathetically.

"God's speed, Johnny-me-boy!" Timothy Devine called after him.

Willy O'Neill, a longtime neighbor, made his deep voice heard over the bustle of the marketplace. "We will be praying for your wife, my friend! I will watch over your stand for you, mark down any sales, and close everything up when day is done."

John nodded his thanks as he lifted Katie up on the rough wooden seat. The ride home was silent and seemed to take a very long time. Katie was afraid to speak because she could see that emotionally her father was barely holding it together as he drove the old workhorse toward home.

As the wagon came to a stop, the doctor was waiting for Katie and her father at the front door. No words were ever spoken. The doctor simply closed his eyes and shook his head.

All Katie remembered was the sound of her father's work boots as he raced across the hard wood floor, and then his cry of heartbreak as he entered their bedroom.

Eliza came up behind Katie and hugged her tightly. "Katie, me darlin', you are a wonderful daughter. You tried so hard to bring Da home in time to say goodbye to Mum. Our Mum just couldna' wait any longer to be with Our Lord."

"I prayed, Eliza!" Katie whispered. "I prayed extra hard so God would save her until Da could say goodbye, but He dinna' hear me!"

"He heard your prayers, sweetheart, but it was time for Mum to leave her pain behind and go home to her heavenly Father. Just picture a beautiful wildflower growing in our yard. We will not pick its blossom until it has reached its peak of beauty. God is just like a gardener. He saw Mum's beauty and picked her from His earthly garden and took her home with Him forever."

"God must really love Mum." Katie sighed. "She will make God happy just like she made all of us so very happy and full of love. But, Eliza, can I still miss Mum even if 'tis God's will to take her to heaven?"

Both girls were startled when they heard their father's voice from behind them.

"We will all miss your Mum for all of our lives. We will feel like a part of our heart is empty. But God will make it easier for us as time goes by; however her loss will always be felt in our heart."

James slowly walked across the floor, joined with his father, and embraced the girls. They stood that way for several minutes, offering comfort to each other.

Finally, their father spoke. "Now, we all have work to do, and it must be completed very quickly. Eliza, you and Katie salt our animals and tell them of Mum's death. Do the salting while on your way to Aunt Bea and Uncle Peter's farm. Please tell your Aunt I would appreciate her help with preparing your Mum. Now, go quickly!"

Eliza rushed to the pantry and grabbed a large tin of salt. "Come, Katie! We dunna' have much time."

"Wait, Eliza!" Katie called. "I dinna' hear a banshee wail and I dinna' see a death coach come to our house for Mum!"

Eliza grasped her sister's hand and flew out the door, intent on their special mission. "No time for explanations, me dear! We have important work to complete and it must be done now!"

The two girls rushed to the paddock and began spreading salt. Katie ran to their cow, Millie, who was staked out in the pasture eating grass. "I am so sorry, Millie, but Da says we must make sure you are salted and purified of bad spirits so Mum can pass to heaven without interference." Katie threw a handful of salt over the cow's head. "Please, Millie, eat my salt as it falls from your head. Sure, it will taste good when combined with your fresh green grass."

Eliza had already salted the two old workhorses and was on her way to the chicken coop when Katie joined her. Together, they salted the rooster and hens and told them the sad story of their Mum's passing. Then, they moved on into the barn to salt the cats.

"I dunna' know if cats count as farm animals," Eliza explained, "but we should make sure and spread salt anyways."

Katie opened the heavy barn door and shouted for each cat by name. Eliza stood in awe as the cats flocked to her sister. "Good job, me darlin'! Now, off we go to tell Aunt Bea."

As the two girls raced through the paddocks, Eliza tried to distract her sister with questions concerning their animals. "I salted two horses, Katie. Did you take care of Millie?"

"All done, Eliza! She must have been salted many times before because she just stood still and continued to chew her cud. Very calm, even when I told her Mum had passed away."

Eliza tried to smile at her little sister. Even though her own heart was breaking, she had to be strong for Katie and the entire family.

"Now, we need to tell Aunt Bea our Da needs her immediate help to get Mum ready for viewing."

Katie looked very puzzled. "What 'tis a viewing?"

Eliza stopped walking and thought for a moment before answering. Death was a very difficult concept to explain to one so young as her sister.

"Well, Katie, all of our neighbors come to our home to say goodbye to our Mum."

Katie interrupted her sister's explanation. "How can our friends tell Mum goodbye when she canna' hear? She certainly canna' answer her friends!"

"No, me sweet," Eliza continued. "Friends and family come and pray for Mum's soul and tell us how sorry for our loss with Mum gone. Everyone will come with food and drink to share."

Now, Katie was totally confused. Tears rolled down her cheeks as she tried to explain the pain in her heart. "Why would we even have a party for Mum when she canna' be with us to share?"

"'Tis a celebration of Mum's life, and everyone will share in our loss of such a great lady." Eliza patiently explained. "Mum gave birth to seven children to carry on our family legacy. She will watch over us from heaven as we strive to be her pride and joy."

Katie was silent for the remainder of the walk to Harrison's farm. While Eliza knocked on her Aunt and Uncle's door, she kept a tight hold on Katie's shaking hand. When Aunt Bea opened the door, she immediately knew that her dear sister-in-law had passed.

Katie flew into Bea's arms. "Oh, Auntie, how will I ever be able to grow up without me Mum? I never was able to say a final goodbye because I ran to market to fetch Da from work. I ran as fast as I could run, and I prayed as hard as I could, but I was too late. Oh, Aunt Bea, I canna' be brave." Katie slid from her Aunt's arms onto the floor, curled herself up into a ball, and sobbed.

Uncle Peter stepped forward, picked Katie up and carried her to his rocking chair. He sat and hugged her tightly until her tiny body stopped trembling.

Suddenly, Eliza remembered her father's request for Aunt Bea's help with her Mum's funeral preparations. "Of course, me dear." Bea quickly responded. "Let us leave Katie here with Uncle Peter and we can take our wagon back to the house. Together, we can wash up your Mum and dress her for the final viewing. We should also send James and Willy for Father Flanagan. Your Mum received *Last Rites* just two days ago, but Father will want to be with all of you and lend comfort and support during this difficult time."

Bea took a moment and studied her niece's face. "'Tis all right to cry, my dear Eliza." Beatrice consoled. "You always try to be strong for everyone else while your own heart is breaking. Shed your tears here, me darlin'. When you are ready, we will both leave together for your home."

Eliza closed her eyes and silently thanked God that her Aunt was taking control and easing the burden from her own shoulders.

The Irish have many unusual customs surrounding the death of a loved one. Leon Uris opens his book, *Trinity*, with the animals on an Irish farm being salted after the death of a family member.

The history of salt is actually very interesting, and dates back to 5,000 BC (even earlier in the Middle East). It was a very valuable commodity and was often used as currency for trade goods.

In the Church, salt was viewed as a purifying agent. There are more than thirty references to salt in the Bible, including Jesus' reference to his own Apostles as *'the salt of the earth.'*

In earlier times, salt was always present on the altar as Mass was said by the priest. Again, signifying purity.

Salting the animals after a death was believed to have *'purified'* the animals of any evil spirits, and would thus allow the soul of the departed to pass overhead with no interference. Centuries ago, family members were expected to salt all animals, as well as every tree on their property in order to secure a safe passage.

Katie mentioned the *Banshee* and the *Death Coach* when speaking to Eliza. These are two very respected parts of Irish folklore.

The Banshee is portrayed as an old woman with long, scraggly white hair, and wearing dark flowing robes. She wails outside the home where a death is imminent, but it is important to note, that the Banshee does not cause actual death, The Halloween witches of today are a good representation of just how the Banshee appeared.

In early Irish history, it was believed that there were two different kinds of Banshees – a good one and a bad one. The good Banshee was a deceased relative that passed away having a loving relationship with her family members. She was clothed in white and did not keen or wail. Her song was uplifting and very supportive. Some references to the good Banshee compare her to a guardian angel.

The bad Banshee died very angry at her family. She wails outside the house and adds unnecessary distress to the grieving family. She was clothed in black with long straggly hair, and keens in a horrible voice. She appears to enjoy her family's pain and loss.

My Grandmother claimed to have heard the Banshee wail on two different occasions – once the night her father died, and the second time when my Grandfather passed.

Today, if you ever have the possibility of seeing a Banshee, she will turn herself into a bird, and all you will hear is the flapping of the bird's wings against the house.

There are stories about individuals that recovered their health and did not pass away after the visit of the Banshee. Actual death does not matter to the Banshee – she simply sends a message to the Death Coach that death could be near.

The story of the Death Coach is entirely different and more frightening than that of the Banshee.

Once the *Death Coach* or *Cóistre Bodhar* (coach-a-bower) is summoned by the cry of the Banshee, it cannot return without a soul on board. The coach is driven by a headless horseman and four black horses. The rumble of the coach gives substantial warning to everyone that death is approaching. Neighbors run from their homes and throw open all the gates in the paddock so that the death coach would have no reason to stop. They shelter in their houses behind locked doors waiting for the sound of the coach to pass by.

One recorded story of the Death Coach occurred in the fall of 1806, in County Claire. The three sons of a very sick man had summoned the doctor and the priest for their father. They waited outside on the door stoop for the men to arrive. When they heard wheels rumbling on the dirt roadway, they ran down to greet the carriage. However, it was neither the doctor nor the priest. Indeed, it was the Death Coach. The boys threw themselves down on the ground in an attempt to hide themselves in the darkness. They were certain the coach had arrived for their father, but were shocked when it did not stop by their home. It seems that the Cóistre Bodhar already had a soul on board ... that of the doctor who had unintentionally crossed paths with the headless horseman!

The term *Last Rites* refers to a sacrament in the Catholic Church that is administered by a priest to a dying congregant. The priest gives the apostolic blessing combined with the anointing with holy oils. It is considered last rites since it is the last time that an individual will receive the blessing.

Anointing of the Sick is the anointing and blessing of a sick congregant in order to bring spiritual and physical strength during an illness. This sacrament can be administered as often as necessary.

Lastly, the term *Extreme Unction* was used in past years instead of last rites. This expression is no longer used in the Church. However, for those interested in Latin roots, *Unction* is translated as *anointing with oils*, while *Extreme* refers to the life-threatening condition of the patient.

CHAPTER SEVEN

♥

Katie sat at the kitchen table, tears streaming down her bright red cheeks. Her sobs echoed through the tiny house, and her words sounded disjointed as she somehow managed to hiccup a question to her sister.

"W...why? She asked Eliza.

Eliza stroked her young sister's back as she struggled to control her own emotions. "Oh, my sweet, it is our circle of life. We are born, we live our lives, and God decides when it is time to take us to His heavenly kingdom."

Katie raised her head and wiped her nose on the sleeve of her favorite sweater. "But w..why?" She asked a second time.

There was no answer that would bring comfort to the brokenhearted child. "Eliza, why are our neighbors eating, drinking, and laughing while our darlin' Mum rests in a pine box?"

"'Tis always been our way, me love. Our neighbors come to celebrate Mum's life with us. Some laugh at her funny adventures, and all cry over her sad losses. All stories are a tribute to Mum, and provide us with memories to last a lifetime."

Suddenly, Mrs. Conley pushed open the thin curtain separating the kitchen from the parlor, and called out to Eliza. "Dearie, you should be greeting your guests and not hiding with your crybaby sister. I will sit with Catherine until your duties are complete."

Eliza paused for a moment. Although Mrs. Conley was correct concerning Eliza's role at the wake, she was also known for her sharp tongue and her thoughtlessness. After some hesitation, Eliza agreed. "I would be pleased to have you sit with Katie, Mrs. Conley". Then she kissed her sister's cheek and assured her that she would return again shortly.

Katie put her face down on the table and softly sobbed. Eliza was her comfort and her strength and she needed her sister by her side.

"Catherine!" Mrs. Conley snapped. "Why are you crying? You are a big girl now, not a baby, so stop your blubbering right now!"

Katie sobbed a little louder as she tried to speak. 'Me Mum ... gone forever!"

"Yes, and me Mum is gone too, but you don't see me bawling for her and carrying on like you!"

"Is your Mum in our parlor getting ready to be buried in the hard cold earth? Did your Mum sing to you and teach you how to play a fiddle while confined to her bed? Did your Mum teach you how to make beautiful lace to help with family expenses? And, did your Mum tell you every day just how much she loved you? Did she, Mrs. Conley? Did she?"

The old woman was very angry with Katie and her eyes were ablaze. "We dinna' have time for such silliness when we were growing up. 'Tis what your head is full of – just silly dreams. Grow up, Catherine!"

Katie stood up from the table, looked directly into Mrs. Conley's eyes, and whispered, "Me Mum wanted me to be called Katie, and I will never forget her love!" By now, Katie's voice had grown a little louder. "I willna' sit at table with such a mean lady as yourself!"

Mrs. Conley had heard more than enough. "Sit down you brazen hussy! If you had never been born, your beloved Mum would be sitting here with me drinking tea and telling stories. You killed her, Catherine! Do you hear me? Your birth led to your Mum's early death!"

James was standing in the kitchen when Mrs. Conley shouted her last words. Katie sat in stunned silence and couldn't believe that she was responsible for her Mum's failing health and ultimate death.

Her brother took hold of both her hands and embraced her very tightly. Then, he turned to address their neighbor. "Mrs. Conley, you have hurt a small innocent child who has done nothing bad in her entire life. Katie truly loved her Mum with all her heart, but I doubt you have ever loved so purely, possessing such a mean spirit. Leave our home immediately, and never dare to enter here ever again!"

Mrs. Conley pushed her large girth up from the table and pounded from the kitchen. When she entered the parlor, all was quiet. The neighbors had heard the hateful things she had shouted at Katie. There would be no forgiveness for this bitter, hurtful woman.

James led his little sister through the parlor and toward the sleeping loft. Each of their friends stepped forward and kissed Katie's cheek, reassuring her that she was a wonderful daughter and deeply loved by her Mum.

James climbed the ladder to the loft and placed Katie on her sleeping mat. He sat and held her hand until she fell into a restless sleep. Then, James silently cried for all the pain his sister endured, as well as his own grief over the loss of his Mum.

One of the beautiful customs of the Irish is the fact that their departed loved ones are never left alone. After the viewing in the home, the pall bearers carry the coffin to the Church the night before the burial. Then, the family members take turns sitting with the deceased praying, or just reliving memories of their loved one. The word *wake* comes from this tradition of family staying *awake* until burial.

Most people have heard stories of the famous *Irish Wake*. Although now outlawed, it was an opportunity for the family to be assured that their family member was truly deceased and not in a coma. While in the coffin, a man would be sat up with a pipe placed between his lips and a glass of whiskey firmly gripped in his hand. Then, if the departed had neither taken a puff on his pipe nor a drink of his Irish whiskey by the end of the night, everyone knew that he had passed.

Before the advent of the heart monitor and today's sophisticated stethoscopes, there was one more strange custom associated with death. A string would be attached to the departed one's toe, and the string would be run outside the pine box and up through the soil.

Then, a family member would attach the string to a bell and sit through the night with a shovel at the ready. If the bell never rang, everyone accepted that their loved one was truly dead.

It has been told that because of this practice, the term *graveyard shift* has now become synonymous with any individual who works a late shift through the night.

It should be noted, however, that these practices did not apply to a woman who had passed. She was not valued as a financial support to the family, and the widower could always remarry another to raise his family and tend the house. Sad, but unfortunately true.

CHAPTER EIGHT

♥

The next morning, Katie awoke to the sound of voices below the sleeping loft. She looked over the edge and saw her two best friends – Nora Scanlon and Marion McGlone – waiting for her to climb down. Katie knew that these two family friends were there to help her through one of the saddest days in her short life.

Nora looked up and saw Katie at the rail. "Well, me sweet, it is time for you to come down and dress yourself for Church. Marion and meself have arrived early to help you look your best!"

Shy Marion smiled up at her beautiful friend. "Me Mum has sent over a new black dress for you to wear. She just finished sewing it late last night."

Katie climbed down the ladder and carefully uncovered the dress from its wrapper. "'Tis simply amazing, Marion! And your Mum used some of my own lace to decorate my collar and cuffs. I wish me Mum could see me in her lovely creation!"

"She will see you from heaven, Katie. And your Mum will be so proud of you!" Marion reached out her arms and embraced her friend. Nora rushed forward and wrapped her arms around both her friends. Together, the three young girls felt comforted and loved being together.

Meanwhile, Aunt Beatrice was organizing everyone in the house and assigning tasks to the neighbors who would prepare the luncheon for all those in attendance. By the time Bea had the arrangements complete, Katie was washed, dressed, and had her long auburn hair braided around her head. Aunt Bea nodded her approval and sent the three girls on their way to the church.

The entire town attended Anne Charlton's funeral Mass, all attired in their Sunday best. Nora and Marion held tightly to Katie's hands as they made their way to the front pews and awaited the arrival of the rest of the family.

Father Flanagan delivered a meaningful eulogy that brought tears to the eyes of the congregation. He explained that Anne was finally at peace and without pain. She would always be looking down on her children as they grew into faithful adults following the precepts of the Church. Although their Mum's life was short, he reassured them that her kind and generous life had earned her an honored place in heaven.

Lastly, Father Flanagan spoke directly to John, the grieving widower. He assured him that God would always be there to guide him and give him the strength that he needed in his new role in the Charlton family.

At that time, the pall bearers stepped forward and shouldered the coffin for the final walk to the gravesite. When Katie reached the cemetery, she released Nora and Marion's hands and looked down into the deep hole that had been dug to accommodate her Mum's pine box.

"No! No!" Katie cried. "They canna' put me Mum in such a cold wet hole in the ground! She will be so cold without even a blanket to wrap around herself. We canna' let Father Flanagan put Mum here for all eternity!"

James stepped forward and lovingly cradled Katie in his arms. "It is only Mum's body we will bury, me sweet. Her soul is already in heaven with God, and she is probably looking down on us right now trying to tell you everything is okay and she is pain free and happy. Now, stop crying, Katie, and maybe you will hear her consoling words to you. Listen carefully, me dear."

Katie immediately stopped crying and prayed along with Father Flanagan as they lowered the coffin. Each of the children stepped forward and dropped a rose on top of the pine box. James was still carrying Katie as she bent over to drop her flower. It was then that she heard a soft whisper. "Do not cry my little one for I will love you forever."

Katie looked up at her brother with a radiant smile on her face. "James, did you hear?" Mum, herself, just told me she would love me forever!"

James kissed his sister on the forehead and set her down on the ground. "Such an honor to have Mum reassure you of her undying love. Treasure it forever, me darlin' Katie."

Then, Nora and Marion rushed forward in order to console their friend. Katie smiled and reassured them that everything was going to be fine. "When I bent down to place a rose on me Mum's coffin, she whispered how much she loves and everything will be okay."

Marion looked to Nora and smiled. "A Mum's love really does go beyond her grave!"

Katie shook her head in agreement. "James helped me to listen for Mum's voice. And now I know that everything is exactly as God wants it to be. And Mum will always be whispering in His ear too!

They slowly walked back toward the house where they met Katie's school friend, Mary Davies, along the road. Mary proudly showed the girls the huge chocolate cake that she had helped her mother make for the Charlton's. "Mum says we are all old enough to learn to bake, and once you are feeling stronger, Katie, she will be happy to give all of us cooking lessons!"

The four girls all joined arms and continued their walk. When they arrived at the cottage, the neighbors were sitting on blankets in the yard enjoying the delicious luncheon that they all worked to prepare. Some of the children were playing games and running in the field, while babies were held in their mother's arms enjoying a rare day of bright sunshine. It was a glorious day and there were no tears, just an outpouring of love.

As the afternoon wore on, the neighbors began to drift off toward their homes. Mary Davies hugged Katie and promised to help her make up any of the schoolwork that she had missed. Katie valued Mary's friendship and the fact that she had such a kind heart.

As the day waned, the crowd thinned until just Marion, Nora, and Katie sat in the yard on the blanket. Marion, however, seemed very nervous and couldn't seem to sit still. Everyone knew that Marion always had a hard time keeping a secret, so Katie assumed that this was the reason for her nervous energy. Nora, her cousin, kept giving her strange looks, almost a warning not to reveal their secret.

Finally, Katie couldn't stand the suspense for one more minute. "All right, Marion, you've been bustin' at your seams to tell me something, so go ahead and tell. I am all ears!"

Nora frowned. "Now is not the time, Marion!" Nora cautioned. "We can wait another day to share our news!"

"Oh no, my friends!" Katie quickly replied. "You canna' keep a secret from your best friend! 'Tis not fair to keep meself from knowing. Please!"

Nora nodded her head indicating that Marion could share their family news.

"Well. Katie, you remember our two brothers have already crossed over to New York in The United States. Both have found very good jobs and are sending money home every month to the family. Now, our boyos are looking to buy two homes very near each other, and send for us to sail abroad. We will finally be reunited as a family once again. Tisn't it wonderful news?"

"No!" Katie shouted. "I just lost me Mum and now I am to lose my two best friends. How will I ever survive living here with only *Crazy Willy* as a neighbor?"

Despite the pain of their future separation, all three girls tried to hide their giggles when Crazy Willy's name was mentioned. They also referred to him as the 'village idiot' due to the fact that he would walk through the woods in all kinds of weather, pieces of paper sticking out of his pocket, while he scribbled notes with a tiny bit of a pencil. He always refused their requests to join in their play, choosing instead to walk and write.

Katie suddenly appeared very serious. She looked at her two friends and felt the tears begin to build in the corners of her eyes. "How soon will you be leaving? Will you both be here for our sixth-grade level?"

This time, Nora chose to answer. "Mum says it might take a year or two to finish collecting all tah money we need to cross. Two of our cousins have already asked to take over our homes, so that makes me parents happy. Mum and Da have asked us to begin sorting all our belongings into two piles – one to donate to children in the orphanage, and a second much smaller pile to take to New York with us."

"New York sounds so very far away!" Katie cried. "Will you forget me after you have been away from Sligo for a short time?"

"We will never forget you, Katie, me dearest!" Marion tearfully whispered. "Both our Mum's say if all goes well for us in America, perhaps you can sail over and be with us."

"That is so true, Katie!" Nora reassured her friend.

Katie hugged the two girls and all three cried together before Nora reminded Marion that it was time they headed back home.

Slowly Katie walked back to the family cottage. When she entered, Katie immediately knew that something felt very wrong. James and her father were sitting at the kitchen table, and it was obvious that their heated conversation had ceased as soon as Katie had entered the house.

"What is going on with both of you? It must be serious if you stop all talk as soon as I enter. Please, do not fight on this sad day. Mum has gone to heaven, and my two best friends are making plans to move halfway around the world. I dunna' know if my heart can take any more bad news!"

James looked at his father, silently urging him to explain the situation to his daughter.

John, however, simply sat rigidly upright in his chair with a stern look on his face.

After several seconds, James realized that it was up to him to explain their conversation. "Katie, before you were born, our oldest brother, John, went to Germany to work on the railroad. Since he left, we have not heard a single word nor received a single shilling from him to help with our family expenses at home. Now, because of Mum's medical expenses and cost of her burial, we really do need help with extra money."

Katie covered her face with her hands and whimpered. James reached out and lifted Katie on to his lap. "Dunna' cry, me little one! It will not be forever. I will come home as soon as I can and we will be a happy ..."

"James!" His father angrily interrupted. "Dunna' be filling your sister's head with lies! Truth be told, James will never return home. He will settle down in another country, make a new home with a wife and raise his own family!"

John continued his rant against his son. "I will not have Katie spending all her days watching our road for you to return home. Just be ready to catch an outbound freighter tomorrow morning and pack lightly!"

John abruptly stood, scowled at his son, and banged the door as he left the cottage. Katie sat on James' lap in stunned silence. Her heart was broken and she couldn't bear the thought of losing her favorite brother. Everyone she loved was leaving her alone in a country where war against the English was on the horizon. James could feel his sister trembling in his arms while he rocked her gently and hummed some of her favorite tunes. Finally, Katie fell asleep with her face buried in the soft wool of his homemade sweater. James stood and carefully carried her up the ladder to the sleeping loft where Eliza waited to help prepare the exhausted child for bed.

William Butler Yeats, the Poet Laureate of Ireland, actually was a neighbor of my Grandmother's. Together with her friends Nora Scanlon and Marion McGlone, they teased him about his strange habit of walking alone in the woods, with bits of paper sticking out of his pockets, always writing. Sometimes, the three girls were so upset with his refusal to play with them, they would throw small stones at him and laugh as he dodged their tosses.

All three women were well into their 80's, and were spending a weekend together at Nora's cottage on Lake Erie. They spent the majority of their time reminiscing about their childhood in Sligo, as well as their adventures in The United States. I was there as their 'gofer,' just in case they needed anything from the store or there was a medical emergency. This also gave me the opportunity to study quietly on the beach for my semester finals. During inclement weather, however, I stayed inside the cottage and listened to their zany stories. One rainy day, Nora casually mentioned the name *Crazy Willy*. The three old women began to giggle like young schoolgirls

I stopped reading and concentrated on their various stories involving a person they referred to as the *village idiot*. When I was finally able to put the pieces of their puzzle together, I calmly asked if they were laughing about William Butler Yeats? All three spoke at the same time and wanted to know how I would ever know his formal name. At that time, I was taking an Irish Lit course, and thankfully I had my copy of Yeats' poetry collection, *CELTIC TWILIGHT,* in my pile of text books. On the cover, there was a large oval containing a photograph of a young Yeats. When I showed the ladies, they howled with laughter. It was Crazy Willy, the village idiot, who lived in the shadow of Ben Bulben.

Nora, was the first to speak, and asked me to read one of his poems aloud. I selected *The Fiddler of Dooney*, one of my light-hearted favorites. They seemed to be impressed by the poem. However, then I made the mistake of telling them that the woods that they played in as children was now renamed *Yeats' Woods*, and suddenly the room erupted in laughter. My Grandmother, who always spoke whatever came to her mind, declared that Yeats was still the same village idiot and crazy Willy they knew from their childhood. After all, Grandmother announced, "a zebra can never change his stripes!"

I didn't have the heart to tell them that Sligo is now the site of *The William Butler Yeats*

Institute, for the study of Irish culture, language, and literature.

Years later, my daughter who was very familiar with her Great-Grandmother's connection with Yeats, wrote her Honor's English thesis on the Irish poet. Her English teacher actually called our home to see if this amusing anecdote was true. After we had spoken about my Grandmother for a lengthy period of time, she suggested that I should write a book about her adventures!

In this chapter, Katie's brother, James, mentions that the oldest of their siblings, John, left Ireland at a young age and traveled to Germany in order earn an income that allowed him to send money home for family expenses. This is true, unfortunately, John was hit by a train while he was working for the railroad and did not survive.

My Grandparents lived with us all of our lives. I was even named after my Grandmother. My parents used to joke that when they said *I do* at the altar, my Grandparents said, *we do too*, and moved right in!

I spent long hours sitting with my Grandmother and learning about her family in the old country, as well as her many adventures in The United States. She even taught me to pray and to swear in Gaelic!

The one thing that I regret is that she was unable to teach me her God-given gift for making lace. You see, I was born left-handed, and Grandmother claimed that I did everything backwards, and she just couldn't figure out how to transpose the patterns or have me hold the needles. Ironically, after her death, I taught myself all the needle crafts – from knitting, crocheting, cross-stitch, and many more – using only my right hand. Even so, her wonderful talent for making lace died with her when she passed away.

Also, I won a college scholarship to study abroad in Ireland at The University College of Dublin Ireland. After classes ended at the University, I spent weeks traveling and meeting all my relatives in Sligo. I even had tea with Mary Davies, my Grandmother's school friend, along with her daughter, Mary provided me with endless stories of my Grandmother's antics!

How I loved my Grandmother Katie, and I still miss her every day of my life.

CHAPTER NINE

♥

The following morning, Katie was awakened by more angry words between James and his father. Her Dad still stubbornly refused to reconsider his decision that James would leave Ireland and pursue a job in Scotland. Both of their voices frightened Katie, and she actually feared they might even come to blows. Finally, however, James grabbed his knapsack and slammed out the door.

Katie jumped down from the sleeping loft and raced out after her beloved brother. "James, please wait just one moment for me! Please, James!"

James stopped walking and turned back toward his sister with open arms. Katie jumped up to meet his embrace straightaway, while James tearfully whispered in her ear, "I will miss you the most, me dear. But I promise I will see you again. And I will pray for you every day and every night." Then, he kissed her cheek as he set her gently back on the ground.

"I will love you forever!" Katie sobbed.

She stood barefoot on the dirt road and watched until James was gone from her sight. *"Please God, protect James wherever he travels. And God, please help me too. Help me broken heart to mend and know me James still loves me no matter how far we are from each other. Amen."*

Katie arrived at their cottage just as Eliza opened the front door. She wiped her tears on the sleeve of her nightshirt before she rushed into Eliza's embrace. Eliza tried to show a stern face when she looked at her sister. "Still in your nightshirt, me girl! And yourself running down our roadway in bare feet too. Whatever would our neighbors say if they saw first-hand your actions?"

Katie looked directly into Eliza's eyes. "I just had to say goodbye to James before he left for Scotland. Da said I would never see him again, so I had to say a proper farewell.!"

Eliza knelt down in the dirt to offer comfort to her sister. Eliza struggled to find the perfect words of encouragement for her sister. However, it was Katie who was the first to speak.

"Who will take care of James while he is so far from home?" Katie asked. "And who will cook for him, do his laundry, and love him the way I do? Who, Eliza? Who?"

Eliza blinked back her own tears as she gathered her thoughts to answer Katie's barrage of questions. "There are no jobs here for James," Eliza began. "Our soil is rocky, so farming is impossible except for growing potatoes. You know the overseer ships almost all our potatoes to tah mainland, and he takes most of the profits for himself. Now, I know of only one job open for James - going out on the ocean every day in treacherous and unpredictable waters to catch fish."

Katie stood straight up with her hands on her hips. "No, not me James! He canna' even fit in his own bed let alone fold his legs up and fit into a curragh!"

Eliza hid her smile behind her hand. James was certainly tall – well over six feet – and totally lacked the coordination to safely row out to sea. Perhaps this fact was the only logical reason that Eliza could offer to effectively justify her father's decision to send James overseas.

"Now, me dearest, please stop all your tears and find something to take your mind off James being gone. Why not concentrate on your new lace patterns to meet all your ever-growing orders at our general store. Many English ladies are waiting to buy some of your beautiful creations, not to mention your rapidly growing orders to make lace curtains."

Katie snarled. "I hate my pieces are purchased by our enemy! English have no right being in our country, taxing what little we have, and claiming our best lands for ..."

"Stop!" Eliza interrupted. "Your political views are only going to get you into serious trouble, Katie. I am not going to stand by and watch British soldiers march you off to prison never to be seen again."

Katie wrapped her arms around herself and squeezed tightly. "You can try to discourage me, Eliza, but soon the Irish people will rise up against British rule and will fight to be free!"

"Enough, Catherine!' Eliza ordered her sister. "Go outside and visit with Nora and Marion, for I can see both girls coming out of our woods."

Katie peeked around her sister in order to see out of the small window. Sure enough, there was Nora and Marion, just when she needed them, headed for their front door.

Katie put a smile on her face, even though it didn't reach her eyes. Then, she bounded out the door calling their names as she ran. "Tell me, did you see Crazy Willy when you cut through our woods?' She questioned her friends.

"Sure, Willy, himself, is out wandering about talking to trees and the same papers hanging out of his pockets." Nora giggled. "He claims he is going to be a famous writer … the most famous in all of Ireland!"

"A famous writer," Marion echoed. "Crazy Willy's head is just full of nonsense! Come on you two, let's play hide-and-seek in the woods near your big apple tree."

All three girls raced out toward the line of trees. Katie temporarily forgot about James' sad departure as she romped and laughed with Nora and Marion. As the sun began its colorful descent into the sea, the friends separated and began their trek homeward.

"Goodbye, me dears!" Katie called over her shoulder. "See you tomorrow!"

Each step that Katie took toward their cottage renewed the pain of James' loss a hundred-fold.

"*Dear God, I am so sorry to bother you again so soon, but please hear my prayer. Take care of me brother, James, and help him to find a good and happy life in Scotland.*" Katie looked heavenward as she continued her prayer, "*And let him know I love him even though I am far away. Please, hear my prayer. Amen.*"

Meanwhile, Eliza was very concerned about her sister's state of mind, and watched from the small window in the door for her return. She breathed a sigh of relief when she caught sight of Katie emerging from the tree line. She waited for Katie to draw near, and then, walked out and embraced her. "Are you feeling better, me dear?"

Katie's eyes flooded over with tears. She found that she didn't have the energy to utter even a few words to Eliza. She swiped at her tear streaked face, gave a weak smile to her worried sister, and then raced into the house and the security of the sleeping loft.

Eliza knew that Katie's heart was broken. The bond that she had with her brother was stronger than with any of her other brothers and sisters. Perhaps they could be reunited at some point in the future, but Eliza's logical side told her that their reunion would never happen. Historically, Eliza knew that the boys who left Sligo in search of work never did return. Their support checks would arrive each month for the first few years, but then they would eventually stop in order to care for their own families.

There had been so much loss in Katie's young life. Her Mum had passed, such a traumatic loss for the youngster. Then, James' forced departure to Scotland, and now Nora and Marion were preparing to move overseas to The United States. Eliza worried about the impact all these events had on Katie. Everyone had already noticed that her sister was much quieter than normal, definitely more withdrawn, and she hardly left the house except to meet her two friends. Eliza was also aware that Katie was dealing with her tumultuous relationship with her father over sending James away from home. Now, Katie practically ignored her Dad, and only spoke to him when she absolutely had to answer one of his questions. The home was eerily silent.

Irish families were often separated due to financial need. The oldest son was usually sent to England, Scotland, or Germany to seek employment.

Scotland was one of the most frequent destinations, since shipbuilding for trade and for pleasure cruising, was such a booming industry.

Daughters were usually sent off to England to work as domestics. Although never respected by the wealthy English class, the maids and kitchen help were still able to earn enough money to send some back to Ireland for financial support.

Also mentioned in this chapter, is the reference to the small window in the door of the Charlton house. Windows were very expensive and a luxury afforded to the rich. Thatched homes that were passed down from generation to generation, usually had only one window, but they also had a front door that was left open whenever possible to allow more light into the house.

CHAPTER NINE

♥

The year was 1916, and *Sinn Féin* (translated *We Ourselves*) along with the *Irish Republican Army* (IRA) were gaining strength all across Ireland. The leaders of this movement were now willing to fight and die for their independence from England.

Katie kept silent about her own involvement in the *cause*. She secretly began to attend meetings with the local rebels. She never dwelled on the consequences of her actions – the fact that she could be tortured, sent to jail without a trial, or even shipped to a penal colony in Australia as a traitor to the crown.

Meanwhile, the Charlton house was very quiet. Eliza's head was buried deep in the pantry taking inventory of their food stores. Katie sat straight in the kitchen chair, biting her lower lip as she concentrated on the new design that she was developing for a lace curtain.

"Are you goin' to be able to meet with Nora and Marion today?" Eliza asked. "We met as I was takin' Da's breakfast to him in market. Both said it was very important to speak with you before Finnigan's barn dance at week's end."

Katie set down her lace on the kitchen table. "Sure, I have no idea what is so important

I must drop everything to meet Nora and Marion. My stitching is not going well, and I have all my deadlines to meet no matter how badly my patterns are goin'. 'Tis just too much pressure on meself and I am not sure I have strength enough to finish all my promised work!"

"Oh Katie, you are just tired," her sister observed. "You are a talented lace maker and I know in just a short time you will figure out how to correct your work. Why not go outside, walk over and call upon your friends. Take some time to unwind, laugh, and have some fun. When you return home, you will be refreshed and ready to solve your pattern dilemma."

Katie stood and removed her apron. "'Tis exactly what I will do, Eliza! Maybe I will get a whole new perspective on what change I need to make in order to improve my pattern.

Then, Katie left the house and took a slow, meandering walk through the woods. Nora and Marion always made her feel better, so she was certain that this visit would do the same. The three girls had a special bond of friendship and love that united them as closely as sisters.

"Hello!" Katie yelled when she first caught sight of her friends sitting in the Scanlon's yard. "You both look very guilty, like the sea bird that just ate the baby puffin! What is up, me dears?"

Nora did not look up and just continued to fiddle with a loose thread on the sleeve of her jacket. Meanwhile, Marion sat looking oblivious to everything around her,

Katie cleared her throat. "Come on you two! Who is going to tell me what is goin' on around here?"

Finally, Marion spoke in a voice barely above a whisper. "Katie, you know we love you like our own sister, always will no matter what happens. However, we just received a letter from our Uncle Ned with all tah money we still need to buy our tickets to America. He says all Irish in his adopted homeland are free to say whatever they want to say. Also, good jobs are available, and once we are citizens, we are guaranteed our right to vote. He wants us to leave Ireland immediately, before any violence breaks out here."

Katie stood silent for a few minutes until she could fully digest what Marion had told her. Katie decided that the best method to use with her friends was to be on the defensive. "You dunna' need to leave Ireland in order to be free. Éamon de Valera is leaving New York City and coming back home with loads of money from his fund-raising tour. He will bring the money and guns to help our cause. Listen, Nora and Marion, our movement has caught on all across Ireland, and I thank the Good Lord. Soon we will be free from English rule."

"We dunna' have time to wait, Katie." Nora attempted to restate the facts sent by her Uncle. "Wireless is reporting that war in Europe is not going very well. Newspapers write about English government going to draft Irishmen to fight in the war. We must leave now, while we still can!"

"No girls, stop and listen to what I have to say!" Katie begged her two friends. "Everyone says America is an answer to all our problems, but how can it be. We already know its streets are not paved with gold like our Grandfathers used to tell us, and how can we all get jobs if the Germans, Italians, Jewish, and Irish people are all heading to America?"

Nora and Marion did not answer Katie's questions. They had no answers, and this made Katie very emotional.

"First, me precious Mum passes away after a long illness. Then, two days later, my Da orders James to go to Scotland and find a job to help pay our bills. Lastly, my two best friends are leaving and traveling half-way around our world to find freedom. Soon, no one will be left in Ireland except the English!"

Katie hung her head to hide her tears. Nora and Marion rushed to her side in order to console her for all her losses. "We will write to you every day," Marion explained. "We will describe everything so you will feel like you are right with us every step of our way."

Nora, obviously very upset with the decision to leave Ireland, attempted to placate Katie. "After we are settled in America, we can make arrangements to bring you over to stay with us."

Nothing could make Katie feel any better about their move. She just nodded her head, too upset to try and speak. She hugged her friends and turned toward home, barely able to see through her tears. Katie did manage to turn one final time before disappearing into the woods. "When would you both be sailing away on your ship?"

Marion looked to Nora to answer Katie's question. "Just two days after Finnigan's barn dance." Nora cried.

"Less than a week to spend with my friends before boarding a ship and setting off for America." Katie forced herself to raise her head and smile at Nora and Marion. "We will make it a week of special memories you can take with you across to America, and keep forever in your heart."

Katie gave one final wave and turned toward home.

Éamon de Valera, was an American by birth. When he was just two years old, his family moved from New Jersey to Ireland.

As a young man, he became involved with the Gaelic League, which was founded in 1893. The goal of the League was to reestablish the Gaelic language and revive pure Irish culture.

Eventually, the Gaelic League became a front for recruiting revolutionaries, and de Valera found himself right in the thick of things.

In 1905, the League gave rise to the Sinn Féin Movement, whose ultimate goal was to set up an Irish Parliament in Dublin.

Left-wing leader, Arthur Griffith, deserves to be recognized alongside de Valera, since he too traveled all across The United States raising millions of dollars for the Irish cause.

In this chapter, Katie mentions *the sea bird that swallowed the baby puffin*. Ireland has a low diversity of breeding birds due to its isolation. However, it should be noted that about half of Greenland's geese and waterfowl winter on the cliffs of the west coast in order to escape the harsh winters of their native country.

CHAPTER ELEVEN

♥

All week, Nora, Marion and Katie prepared for the barn dance at Finnegan's farm. This was an annual event that the entire county looked forward to after the long cold winter.

The barn was swept clean, bales of hay were put in place for seating, and lanterns illuminated by candle light hung from every beam to ensure that the dancing would continue long into the night.

New dresses were laid out and Eliza had volunteered to style the hair of all three girls. No one had new shoes to wear since they were so dear. Even Mrs. McGlone made each of the girls a new dress. Although made from the same pattern, different material was utilized for each one. Katie's dress was bright yellow with a fitted white bolero to accent her tiny waist. She just couldn't believe the amazing outfit that Marion's Mum had sewn just for her.

"Well Katie," Marion asked, "how does your new dress fit yourself?"

Katie twirled around the kitchen. "Begorrah, Marion! 'Tis perfect and even spreads out into a huge circle when I twirl!"

"Well, twirl yourself over here so I can comb out your hair," Eliza ordered.

"Can I wear my hair up in a fancy twist like all the sophisticated ladies?"

Eliza scowled. "No, you certainly may not! You are not old enough to be wearing such styles. Maybe, I should just plait your hair in pigtails and tie each one with a ribbon, just like when you were a young schoolgirl!"

Katie looked down at the floor and stuck out her lower lip in a mock pout. "Do not hide your face, young lady because I can still see your playful twinkle in your eyes! You are not fooling anyone with your silly request. And, Miss Katie, I willna' ever give in to your ridiculous pouting face!"

All three girls laughed at Eliza's serious tone of voice. They knew Katie was always trying to make her laugh with her silly faces.

Eliza ignored their laughter and continued to style Katie's hair. She had even purchased fancy hairclips from the general store to keep their hair from falling into their faces when they danced with all the anxious young men.

As soon as Eliza finished Katie's hair, she sent her over to the mirror that she had propped up in the corner of the kitchen.

"Oh, Eliza, I canna' believe what you have done! I look like a princess with me long auburn tresses draped down me back! And your beautiful hairclips are truly frosting on the cake – a perfect touch! Tank you, me love!"

Marion was next in line. She was so thrilled with the completed style that she hugged and kissed Eliza with tears in her eyes.

"I will give back your clips at tonight's conclusion. I canna' tell you how pleased I am with what you have done for meself!"

Eliza was emotional as she addressed Katie's two friends. "I dunna' want me clips back from either of you. Please take me gift with you to America as a reminder of how much we love you and how much we will always miss you!"

All four of the girls became very weepy and stood hugging each other tightly - never wanting to let go. With all the festivities surrounding Finnegan's barn dance, they had temporarily forgotten that in just two days they would be separated forever!

Eliza was the first to compose herself. "Sure, enough with all our tears! Now, 'tis Nora's turn to have her hair styled before we leave for Finnegan's.

Nora's striking red hair glowed in the firelight. Her curls cascaded down her back after Eliza loosened them from her tight bun. Nora could have cared less how she looked. As a matter of fact, Nora would have been more comfortable in her old coveralls and a simple braid. She was totally unaware of just how attractive she actually had become.

Eliza lined up the three friends for final inspection, and smiled proudly. "You girls are truly a sight for sore eyes ... stunning! I bet all our young men will be lined up waiting for a chance to dance with each of you!"

Finally, it was time to leave for Finnegan's. The farm was not very far from the Charlton's home, so they decided to walk instead of riding in the horse and cart. The three girls never stopped jabbering throughout the walk. Eliza stayed slightly behind them, marveling at the range of topics they discussed during their stroll.

As they approached the barn, they saw that the yard and the pastures were already filled with wagons, while the sound of jigs and reels filled the air. Eager to take part, the three girls picked up their pace and ran to the open barn doors.

"Look how lovely everything looks!" Nora shouted over the music! Paddy Conlon of Tobercurry is playing his fiddle and he is so talented. Me Mum says he even makes his own fiddles!"

"Does he come from a large family?" Katie inquired as she listened to his music and tapped her feet to the irresistible beat.

"Oh, yes! His handsome brother, John, has already shipped off to America and is doing very well as a trolley car conductor. His younger brother, Michael, wants to join him as soon as possible. Paddy also has a married sister and two other brothers."

Meanwhile, Marion had noticed the long tables filled with bowls of punch and every kind of cookie imaginable. She tugged on Katie's hand

and pointed to the first table. Katie in turn, grabbed on to Nora's hand and they headed off in that direction. Before they even reached the first table, Katie was whisked away to the dancefloor by Sean Murray. In just a matter of minutes, both Nora and Marion were asked to dance, and joined Katie and Sean on the crowded dancefloor.

Paddy Conlon played faster and faster until the step-dance came to a sudden end. Everyone cheered for the talented fiddler before they rushed off to the punch bowls.

"Tisn't his music wonderful?" Katie asked her friends as she wiped her brow with her handkerchief. "Paddy Conlon is so gifted. I wish I could take even one fiddle lesson from him. I could learn so much! Just think, I could become a famous woman fiddler in Sligo County!"

Nora and Marion looked at their friend and giggled. Katie was already a gifted musician and her reputation was growing in leaps and bounds.

Later that evening, Nora gasped and pointed toward the raised platform that was serving as a stage. "Look!" Nora cried. "Paddy is smiling and signaling he wants you, Katie, to come forward."

Katie turned toward the platform in total disbelief. Paddy was pointing directly at her and motioning for her to come up on the stage. Katie grabbed on to both Nora and Marion's hands and timidly approached.

"Well, Katie Charlton, how about sharing me stage with an old man and playing together?" He grinned at all three young ladies. "I have an extra fiddle and I would be honored if you would join me playing and singing tah *Parting Glass*. But first you will have to let go of your friends' hands so you can tune your fiddle!" Paddy laughed at his own joke. "You already are familiar with tah music, so jump on up and let's get our act together!"

Suddenly, the barn became very quiet as the guests realized that young Katie Charlton was going to share the stage with the talented Paddy Conlon. Katie adjusted the fiddle for comfort and held it in place using her chin rest. Then, she carefully tightened the strings on the bow, smiling up at Paddy as she completed the pre-play ritual. "I will follow you, sir, if you just give me a count."

Together, they began the opening bars of the traditional *Parting Glass*. Katie's voice was strong but sweet as she began to sing. Paddy just winked his eye and grinned his pleasure at the talented young girl. On the last verse, the entire congregation joined in with Katie, raised their glasses and sang:

"*So fill to me the Parting Glass, goodnight and God be with you all*!"

The crowd erupted into loud applause, whistles and hoots. Katie was visibly shaken when she looked out on the crowd and watched her Dad wipe a tear from his eye. Katie realized that he was proud of her, and for the first time since her Mum died years before, Katie felt close to her father again.

Then, the dance was over and it was time to walk home. Katie had a hard time moving through the crowd since everyone wanted to congratulate her and shake her hand after her brilliant performance. Nora and Marion stayed close to their friend. They didn't want the evening to end and be forced to say goodbye forever to sweet Katie Charlton.

"Come my talented beauty!" Her Dad encouraged her. "We must say farewell and best wishes to both Scanlon's and McGlone's. Sure, a new life is awaiting all in America."

Katie stopped dead in her tracks. For the past week she had tried so hard to keep her emotions in check, but now there was no way to escape their final goodbyes. When she looked to Marion and Nora, their eyes were filled with tears.

It was Nora who broke the painful silence. "Sure, we will both write letters to you as soon as we get settled. We will use our words to paint vivid pictures of New York for you, me dear."

Marion stepped forward and pressed her lucky stone into Katie's hand. Marion had carried this special stone with her since childhood and truly believed in its 'sometime' magical powers. "You take care of me lucky stone, Katie, until we see each other again in America!"

Eliza quickly reached out and took Katie's hand, offering the emotional support that she knew her sister desperately needed. As if rehearsed, her father gently took hold of her other hand, reassuring her that she was not alone and that she was profoundly loved by all despite her heartfelt loss.

The song entitled *The Parting Glass* was originally written by an Irishman who returns to his neighborhood pub to say a final goodbye to all his friends – since he is about to die.

Over the years, it became the last song of the evening. Everyone would raise their glasses and sing. It was always an emotional end to an evening shared with loved ones and friends.

My Great Uncle Paddy Conlon was indeed a very talented fiddler and played at barn raisings, dances, weddings, and parties of all kinds. Additionally, he did make his own instruments, although none of my family members in America were fortunate enough to possess one.

Ironically, our two daughters are concert violinists and play in two prestigious orchestras. We are always asked if either my husband or I play, but the answer is always a firm *no*! Their talent comes from our Irish family ... especially Great Uncle Paddy Conlon!

CHAPTER TWELVE

♥

Once Nora and Marion left Ireland, Katie found herself truly alone for the first time in her life. Since their neighbor, Liam McDermott, began courting her sister, even Eliza was hardly ever at home. In an effort to avoid total boredom, Katie threw herself into her needlework and began producing some of the most intricate lace that she had ever made.

The English ladies lined up to place their orders from the talented young woman. Katie always treated the aristocracy with the greatest respect when they came to place their orders; however, after they departed, she harshly criticized herself for conducting business with the enemy.

It was late winter, 1916, and the Irish revolutionaries had become a force to be reckoned with by the English. Additionally, the Irish that had emigrated to The United States, were now supporting the uprising with millions of dollars. Katie secretly continued to attend meetings of either Sinn Féin or The Irish Republican Army. No one at home even suspected that she was sneaking off in the afternoon or the early evenings to attend the subversive meetings.

One afternoon, Eliza was home and decided to prepare lunch for her sister before she left to meet Liam. She looked around for Katie, but she was no where to be found. Eliza even walked to the edge of the woods and called out her name – but to no avail. It was then that Eliza wrote a note to her sister and propped it up against her covered meal.

Just as Eliza was walking out the door, she spied Katie at the edge of the woods with James Connolly. A very handsome and young-looking man, Connolly was a known rebel and was constantly under scrutiny by the British army. Eliza was furious! Her sister was fraternizing with an enemy of the Crown.

Katie approached the cottage with a welcoming smile on her face. "Eliza, me dear, dunna' leave before you meet me friend, James."

Eliza gave Katie an angry glance before addressing James Connolly, himself. "I know who Mr. Connolly 'tis, but what 'tis he doing with my sister?"

Katie frowned and was about to speak, when James put his hand on her shoulder in order to silence her. "Good afternoon, Miss Charlton." James addressed Eliza. "I am simply walking your sister home after one of our meetings. We had so much to talk about, I decided to escort Miss Katie and discuss our plans for our Irish free state."

Now, Eliza was absolutely livid. "So, you believe you can just talk to Katie and take advantage of her young mind? Are you trying to convince her to be a part of your rebellious movement?" Eliza, red-faced and distraught, continued to rattle off her questions. "Does it even matter to you if Katie is captured by British soldiers? And are you intent on using my sister until she is shipped off to a penal colony in Australia? You are not welcome here, Mr. Connolly, and I want you to stay away from my sister!"

Katie was shocked by Eliza's harsh and hateful words. She had never heard Eliza speak to anyone in such a disrespectful way. However, it did not seem to intimidate James Connolly – he simply bent down, kissed Katie's cheek, and turned back toward the woods.

"How could you be so rude to my friend?" Katie shouted. "Sure, I am embarrassed for poor James!"

"Embarrassed for a rebel?" Eliza continued her rampage. "You sneak off to his meetings to help him plan a revolution and no one even knows where you are or if your life is in peril. You keep company with known enemies of the English government as if you're playing a game with friends. And you even dare to bring one to our home. What is wrong with you, Katie? How is Da goin' to feel when I tell him what has happened here today?"

Katie turned toward the house and began to walk away. Just before she reached the door, Katie turned one final time and faced Eliza.

"I will not give up my feelings concerning a free Ireland. I am ready to fight for our cause – even ready to give me life for freedoms we deserve!"

Katie entered the house and slammed the door on her sister. When Eliza entered, Katie was up in the sleeping loft reading a pamphlet that she had hidden in her pocket. Eliza never said another word to her sister. She settled down in her Mum's rocking chair and waited for her father's late return from work. She was determined to discuss everything in detail with her Dad. Soon he would know about his young daughter's illicit involvement with the rebels.

It was well after sunset when John Charlton returned from the marketplace. He was totally exhausted and felt a definite tightness in his chest. He placed his horse in the barn, and physically struggled to brush him down, feed, and then water the old workhorse. When completed, he literally dragged himself to the house, sadly recalling the small amount of money he had earned for a twelve-hour day. Not only that, but his sales had been in a freefall for the last several months and he had no answer why this was happening.

As soon as John entered his home, he sensed that something was horribly wrong. Eliza appeared to be in a terrible state of mind.

"'Tis everything all right?" He questioned his oldest daughter.

Eliza began to relate the events of the afternoon and Katie's secret involvement with the rebels, when suddenly, John grabbed hold of his left arm and fell to the floor. His face was ashen in color, and his eyes closed, with no movement whatsoever.

Eliza screamed, and Katie quickly jumped down from the loft.

"Go for help, Katie! Take Da's horse and fetch Doctor Keighron as quickly as you can! Go now!"

Within seconds, Katie was bareback on her father's horse, galloping toward town. When she saw a tall man walking in her direction, she slowed for just a second to ask for help. Katie was shocked to see that the stranger was actually her brother, James, home from Scotland.

"Go quickly, James, and help Da!" She cried. "He is sick and I must fetch Doctor Keighron from town."

"Go, me love, with God's speed!" James called over his shoulder as he ran toward the cottage. He burst through the door and found Eliza trying to pick up their father from the floor.

"Wait, me darlin'!" James advised his sister. "I will pick up Da and carry him to his bedroom if you rush ahead and turn down tah bedding."

John was not conscious at this time, and James could barely detect a pulse at his father's wrist. "Whatever has happened here?" John whispered to his sister.

Eliza sat in the chair next to the bed, and told him of Katie's involvement with the rebels. She also told her brother that of late, everyone seemed to avoid their father's fish stand and, therefore, money was very tight.

James bend close to his father's ear. "Da, can you hear me? 'Tis James, and I would like you to open your eyes if you can hear me. Please, Da!"

John did open his eyes and was very surprised to see his son right there in front of him. "James, me boy, how I have missed you!"

"Rest now, Da, and we will take care of everything for you. No worries for you to bother yourself about."

He watched as his father closed his eyes and rested. Then, Eliza and James left the room so that they could speak freely.

"Why are you home, James? And tell me how long you will be able to stay with us?"

James wrapped his arms around his sister as he related the recent events in his life. He only had one week to visit, but he wanted to return home to Ireland and tell his family that he had met a wonderful Scottish colleen, Mary Jane, and they were going to be wed.

Eliza was speechless, but she stood up on her toes and kissed her brother's cheek. She was so happy that James had found love in Scotland. Before she could ask her brother about his specific plans for the future, the front door flew open and Katie arrived, followed by the doctor.

James stepped forward and escorted Doctor Keighron into his father's bedroom. Then, he returned to the kitchen to sit with Eliza and Katie.

"I believe it will be a long night for all of us," he advised, "so Eliza, please fill your kettle for tea. Katie, place some biscuits on our table in case tah doctor would like something with his tea."

Both girls sprang into action, so relieved that James was home to take the burden from their shoulders.

Eliza pumped the kettle full and carried it to the fireplace. Katie busied herself with arranging shortbread cookies on one of her Mum's favorite plates. Then, the three siblings sat at the table, holding hands and praying for their father.

The doctor finally emerged from the sickroom and sat down at the table to discuss their father's failing health. He took a sip of tea before he began his explanation. "Your Da has suffered a severe heart attack. His heart is so weak, it will surely be a miracle if he lasts more than a day or two at most. Please keep him very quiet with no excitement to hasten his passing. I have known about John's heart condition for many years, and I have warned him against his long and dangerous hours at work. His lifestyle would definitely lead to his demise. But you know your father! He refused all me medical advice. His only concern was to support and take care of his family."

The doctor paused for a moment to study the faces of John's devoted children. "Your Da has asked to see Katie for just a few minutes, and I told him I would send her in right away. James, I believe you can help your sister emotionally if you go into the bedroom with her."

James took his sister's delicate hand in his large calloused one, and walked with her into the darkened room.

"Da?" Katie whimpered. "Do you want to talk to me?"

John opened his eyes, looked up at his youngest daughter and smiled. "Oh, Katie me darlin', I want you to know how much I love you and want you to be happy after I am gone. Me heart has been sick for a long, long time, and I knew I would be leaving you shortly. You must never feel guilty for my passing – it is me time to be with your Mum again, and I am very peaceful and happy. Just know in your heart, I will always love you."

Katie lowered her head to her father's chest while he gently stroked her hair. "Da, you just need a little rest. Sure, a little rest and you will be right as rain."

John looked up at James and conveyed with his eyes that it was time to bring Eliza and the rest of his children into the room to say goodbye.

When all were gathered around their father's bed holding hands and gently weeping, John smiled at each of them individually, closed his eyes and peacefully passed away.

Dr. Keighron entered the room and whispered to James that he would stop at Bea and Peter's house to let them know that John had passed. Then, he would stop at the wood smiths to send out a pine box.

Katie refused to leave the chair beside her father's bed. She sat and cried, watching as the tears splashed upon their clasped hands.

The remainder of the family quickly went about to salt the animals and tell of their father's death.

Soon, Bea and Peter arrived to prepare the body. Once again, Katie refused to release the grasp on her father's hand. Finally, James pried open her fingers and led her from the room.

Word traveled quickly that there was a death at the Charlton cottage. Neighbors arrived with food and flowers for the family. Katie, however, had moved a kitchen chair next to her father's coffin and sat silently as she continuously fingered her rosary and prayed for the repose of her father's soul.

James Connolly was elected Commander-in-Chief of the Irish insurgents. He worked closely with the Irish Republic's newly elected president, Patrick Pearse.

It was Connolly who negotiated with the Germans to deliver a large shipment of guns and ammunition to the west coast of Ireland on Good Friday, April 21, 1916.

The Germans, who were part of the Triple Alliance (Germany, Austria-Hungary, and Italy) during World War I, were delighted to help the rebels defeat their enemy during the height of the war. All the plans that Connolly so skillfully formulated were thwarted when the British captured the German vessel.

CHAPTER THIRTEEN

♥

John Charlton's wake and funeral were extremely difficult for Katie. Her two best friends, Nora and Marion, were no longer living in Ireland, and she desperately missed their strength and comfort.

Eliza bravely carried through all the rituals with the assistance of her fiancé, Liam, while James handled all the formalities. He even insisted on shouldering his father's coffin to his final resting place. In the procession, Katie was left all alone walking behind the pall bearers.

After the ceremony, the crowd of townspeople slowly walked back to the Charlton house for refreshments and a luncheon. Katie gently refused all James' offers to walk her home. All she wanted was to spend time by herself at the gravesite.

Katie bowed her head and spoke to her father. "I canna' believe you are gone, Da! I always imagined we would have more time together, but obviously, God had different plans for you. I will miss you just as I still miss Mum, and I will never forget both of you. Your bodies may be side-by-side in dirt, but I know you are both dancing together in heaven. Mum will be healthy, and your heart will be healed."

Katie lowered her face into her hands as she prayed. "I will see you again Mum and Da. I will see you together in heaven. Amen!"

James, who had remained at a distance to give Katie the privacy that she needed, now advanced toward the new grave. "Begorrah, Katie!" James whispered. "Come take me hand and let us walk home together. Da and Mum are no longer here on our earth, but at peace together in heaven. Let us go and celebrate life with our family and friends.

Katie took her brother's hand and began the walk in silence. She knew that James would soon be returning to Scotland to marry Mary Jane and begin his new life. Eliza, too, would walk down the aisle of their tiny church to become Liam's wife, while Mary, Michael, and Willy had already returned to southern Ireland to resume their employment in the Waterford Crystal factory. Suddenly, Katie felt so desperately all alone.

James spent most of that day with his sister, making sure that she did not go off by herself to mourn. She stood silently next to James as he said goodbye to each of their friends and neighbors. The guests could see that John's youngest daughter was heartbroken, so they took time to repeat their sympathies and pledges of prayer. Katie appeared to be in a daze as she nodded her gratitude.

Later that evening, James lit a fire and sat down in his father's chair, while Eliza rocked in her Mum's. Earlier, Katie had expressed her desire to speak with them concerning her future plans, and they anxiously awaited her decision.

"I know both of you have made plans for your lives and I willna' be a burden to either of you." Katie began in a strong voice. "I have one more promise to keep before I can be off to America. Nora and Marion have secured employment for me as a maid with a very rich family, and Mrs. McGlone has offered me a bedroom for use on my days off from work. All my plans seem to have fallen into place at a perfect time in me life."

"No, Katie!" Eliza cried. "You canna' leave, for surely me heart would break."

Katie looked directly into Eliza's eyes. "You have a new life with Liam and no place for a younger sister to interfere with newlyweds. James will also begin his new life with his beloved Mary Jane far off in Scotland. I dunna' really have a place here anymore."

Katie wiped a tear from her eye with her shirtsleeve. Without a second thought, James reached into his pocket and retrieved his handkerchief. Katie studied the monogramed piece of cloth closely. "I sew much better now, James. This was one of my very first pieces I ever made."

"I carry it with me always, me darlin'," James admitted. "It was a very special gift you made, and it reminds me of you every time I take it from me pocket."

Katie smiled at her brother, and then continued explaining her plans for the future.

"I have saved enough money from my handcrafts to buy a ticket onboard ship to New York. Nora and Marion are in a town called Buffalo, and both have made all my arrangements once I arrive.

James paused for a moment before he spoke. "Sounds like you have wonderful plans in place once you reach Buffalo. We owe both Scanlon and McGlone families our deepest gratitude. I dunna' have any problems with your plans, Katie, but why not leave now so I can go with you to your ship, and wave goodbye as you set off for America?"

"I canna' leave just now, James. You see, I have one more task to complete before departure. I canna' tell you what it is, but I must keep my word."

Eliza frowned. "Tell me, does your promise have anything to do with Mr. James Connolly?"

Katie smiled at the sister who had so lovingly raised her since birth. "Eliza, me darlin', I canna' tell you what I have promised. I will never put my friends' lives in jeopardy. Just have faith in me, trust me , and know I am making all me decisions for Ireland's benefit."

James stood and took Eliza's hand. He knew that she feared for Katie's future and the danger she faced by joining with the rebels. James, on the other hand, felt the same way that

Katie did, and knew it was time for Ireland to rise up against the English, fighting for a free country.

"We will stand by your decision to leave after Easter, me dear. It will surely break our heart to know you are so far away, but we must remember you are old enough to make your own decisions." James continued to hold Eliza's hand as they walked to the center of the room and embraced Katie.

Time seemed to pass very quickly until the day for James' departure arrived. On that particular day, James spent every minute possible with Katie. As they walked through the woods, they discussed all their hopes and dreams for the future. They even stopped to watch Crazy Willy as he ambled through the trees scribbling notes on his tiny scraps of paper.

"I believe Crazy Willy will always be here in our woods, totally unaware of all that is goin' on around him." James voiced with a hint of laughter. "Just Willy and his writings together forever."

Katie giggled. "Sure, he will never make anything of himself. He lives a lonely life here with his Grandmother, while his Mum is off livin' her life in England. I truly feel sorry for him after all Nora, Marion, and meself did. We teased and taunted poor Willy, and made him suffer."

"We all have many events in our lives to be sorry for, especially when we grow older and look back on what we have done to others."

James paused for a moment and gazed up at the sky. "I am so sorry about all my arguments with Da about having to leave home to find work. We reconciled before he passed, but I still carry scars on me heart. I loved him so much, but I never took time to tell him."

Katie fought to control the tears that were threatening to fall. Once again, James reached into his pocket and retrieved the handkerchief Katie had made for him. "Now, you know why I never leave home without your special gift. So, dunna' cry and make it soiled before I leave on me ship!"

"Oh, James, how I punished Da for sending you away. I dinna' talk to him unless I absolutely had to, and my voice always sounded mean when I did respond. I forced him to eat his supper alone, even after he came home exhausted from one of his very long days at work. Sure, it is only lately we were able to mend our fences."

"Well, Katie, be grateful you forgave Da and had a great reunion with him before the Lord called him home." James attempted to console his sister. "Forgiveness is a very fine gift to give another!"

James pulled his father's watch fob from his vest pocket and checked the time. "I must be goin' me darlin' Katie. I have a boat to catch come evening, so I must be on my way."

Petite Katie stood high on her tiptoes and kissed her brother's cheek. "I love you, James, with all me heart, and someday I know we will be together again."

James wiped the tears in his eyes with the same handkerchief he had lent to Katie. Then, he carefully folded his treasured gift and placed it in his breast pocket, kissed his sister one final time, turned and headed for the docks.

In olden days, wakes were very different from how we view our deceased today. Men stayed in the same room as the coffin, while the women congregated in the kitchen and *keened* for the departed. Keening is a high-pitched wail of sorrow, very mournful and not a pleasant sound.

When my Dad passed away at a very young age, my Grandmother, his mother-in-law, made a horrible, mournful sound that made my blood run cold. I had never heard the sound of someone keening, and I hope that I never hear that sound again.

One interesting fact about my Grandmother is that she never believed in using tissues for her needs. She always carried a linen handkerchief in the deep pocket of her apron. She taught me that ladies never left the house without their homemade handkerchiefs - always hand-tatted around the edges and embroidered with initials or designs. To his day, I never leave the house without one in my purse!

CHAPTER FOURTEEN

♥

Finally, after serious deliberation, Eliza and Liam formulated a plan to help Katie overcome her sense of loss and deepening depression. The answer was actually quite simple - they would offer to attend, with Katie, one of James Connolly's rallies in Sligo Town.

Eliza waited patiently for her sister to return from delivering her lace to the general store. "How did you make out with your sales?" Eliza inquired. "Do you have anything new to tell me?"

"Same as always. Nothing special, except I was surprised to see even more orders for my lace curtains."

"Why would you be surprised, me darlin'? Your lace is finest in all of Ireland!" Eliza tried desperately to raise her sister's spirits with her compliment.

"I really believe now is my time to take all my savings and travel to New York to see Nora and Marion. I am not happy here, Eliza. All my days blend together and I have nothing to look forward to in my life."

"Will you stay for my wedding to Liam? And will you still be here for our first Easter Sunday as husband and wife?"

Katie was surprised to see tears in her sister's eyes. Eliza was always the strong one in the family and never revealed herself as over-emotional.

"Of course I will stay for your wedding, Eliza! What kind of sister would I be if I dinna' walk down tah aisle as your Maid of Honor?"

Eliza hugged Katie tightly. Finally, her sister had committed to be a part of her wedding – a topic that Katie had purposely avoided for weeks.

"I have a surprise for you, little sister. I heard your friend, James Connolly, is leading a rally in town tonight. Would you like to attend with Liam and meself?"

Katie's smile lit up the room. Eliza breathed a sigh of relief knowing she had made the right decision concerning the rally.

"Oh, Eliza, I love you so much for changing your mind about James and his mission. You will hear him outline exactly what his plans are to force England to give us our freedom. You will not be sorry you decided to attend!"

"Liam and I will only attend one meeting, Katie. We will listen to what Mr. Connolly has to say, but we will not take part in his revolution. Most important, Liam and meself can both be present to watch over you and make sure no one will arrest you for taking an active part in an illegal gathering."

Katie didn't seem to care what reason Eliza gave for attending Connolly's rally. Katie, herself, was going to Sligo Town with her sister and fiancé to hear James Connolly fire up the crowd and attract more supporters to the cause. Katie believed that this could be a real turning point for Eliza's conversion to the freedom movement.

Liam arrived with his wagon and waited patiently for the two women to finish their preparations for the short trip into town. Desperate to get underway, Liam opened the front door and yelled that time was running out and they had to get underway immediately or they would miss the opening speakers. No sooner were the words out of his mouth, than Eliza and Katie were out the door and climbing up onto the wagon.

Katie was so excited that she never stopped rambling on and on about what they were about to hear. Liam gave Eliza a quick glance and a wink as he drove the wagon over the rutted roadway. Eliza smiled and affectionately rubbed her husband's arm; however, Katie was lost in her own world of revolution, and never noticed their signs of deepening love.

At the end of the night, Eliza had to admit that Connolly was a gifted speaker. She could agree with many of the points that he made, but could not support violence to any degree. Both Liam and Eliza believed that arbitration and meaningful peace talks could negotiate an end to the harsh English laws.

On the other hand, Katie had stars in her eyes at the end of the rally. James Connolly finished his address, and amid cheers from the crowd, he walked down shaking hands with his followers as he made his way directly up to Katie. He kissed her cheek and then took her hand as they walked back to Liam's wagon. James smiled at Eliza and then lifted her up to the roughhewn seat of the old wagon. Eliza acknowledged his courtesy with a curt nod. Then, he lifted Katie onto the seat next to her sister. Katie reached down and tenderly touched Connolly's cheek before Liam drove away.

"What is going on between James Connolly and yourself, Katie?" Eliza questioned. "You are a beautiful young lady and I believe that he is smitten with you!"

Katie simply smiled and gave no answer to her sister. She knew that James was a good man who was ready to give his life for Ireland's freedom. Although Katie's heart raced when she listened to James speak, there was no romantic feelings between the two of them. Katie knew that she would avoid any relationship with a revolutionary. Always on the run from the authorities, always looking over your shoulder to make sure that you were never followed, and always living with the fear of extreme punishment for their activities ... this was not the life that she wanted to live. Katie looked forward to marriage, managing her own home, and eventually having children.

As the three began their journey home, Katie placed her head on Eliza's shoulder and nodded off to a dreamless sleep.

James Connolly was born in Edinburgh, Scotland in 1868. He was the founder of the Irish Socialist Party, and an advocate for Ireland's freedom from British rule.

Connolly partnered with Patrick Pearse, plus one thousand of their volunteers, to take control of several strategic buildings in Dublin's city center on Easter Monday, April 24, 1916.

The most famous of these buildings was the General Post Office or the GPO. This massive structure still dominates O'Connell Street, at a major intersection in downtown Dublin.

Today, the GPO is viewed as a historic reminder of Ireland's failed Easter Rebellion of 1916.

If visiting Dublin today, you can still view the bullet holes on the exterior of the General Post Office, and it is considered one of the top ten attractions in Dublin.

CHAPTER FIFTEEN

♥

The morning of Eliza's wedding, the sun was brightly shining and the rain that fell during the night had all but dried from the dirt roadway.

Katie was dressed in a pale pink, floor-length gown that Eliza had sewn for her. Her auburn hair was twisted and styled atop her head. However, she found herself very nervous and constantly wore a path back and forth in front of the fireplace.

Finally, when Aunt Bea and Uncle Peter arrived, Bea only tolerated Katie's pacing for a short period of time. "Katie, sit down and stop adding to your Uncle Peter's nervousness."

It had been previously determined that Peter would escort Eliza down the aisle since both her Dad and Mum had passed.

Peter smiled at his niece. "Looks like we both have a bad case of nerves!" He admitted. "Maybe we should sit together and give each other a little courage!"

Katie looked at her Uncle and softly whispered her apologies as she sat down next to him at the kitchen table.

All three stood when they heard the sound of the downstairs bedroom door open and Eliza emerged. Katie gasped and then began to weep at the sight of her sister. Eliza stood before them wearing her Mum's wedding gown – so beautiful and the perfect picture of her mother.

Katie could feel her heart beating fast as she tried to speak. "Eliza!" She gasped. "Sure, you are the most stunning bride I have ever seen, and a flawless image of our Mum!"

"I whole-heartedly agree!" Aunt Bea chorused.

Uncle Peter walked to Eliza and lovingly whispered in her ear. "I am so proud to take your Da's place and escort you down the aisle." Eliza embraced him tightly and tried hard to blink back the tears that threatened to flow from her eyes.

Peter tucked Eliza's hand into the crook of his arm as they began the short walk to the church. Beatrice took Katie's hand and held tightly as they slowly followed behind Peter and the bride.

When they arrived outside the door of the church, Aunt Bea entered to take her place in the front row, and signaled the music to begin. Katie slowly stepped off, with Eliza and Uncle Peter directly behind her.

The entire congregation stood and smiled at the wedding party as they processed up the aisle. Katie was moved by all the love she felt from their family and friends, and lovingly returned the sentiments.

Liam stood before the altar. His smile was radiant and reflected all the love he felt for his beautiful bride as she approached. These two individuals had waited a long time for this day to come. Now, they tenderly professed their deepest feelings and devotion to each other in good times as well as times of sorrow, 'till death they do part.

Now, the reception began, with all the neighbors bringing the food they had prepared for the happy couple. Irish whiskey and Guinness Stout flowed while the quests enjoyed the repast.

The newlyweds departed shortly after supper, but the guests stayed late into the night. Katie had hidden her fiddle under one of the tables, and now stood before the group carefully tuning its strings against the dampness.

The Charlton family and friends raised their glasses and sang *The Parting Glass* with Katie. This officially signaled that the celebration was now complete.

Everyone clapped and cheered before they slowly made their way back to their cottages.

Traditionally, wedding gowns were passed down from one generation to the next. Although it saved the cost of making a new dress, it was the love of tradition that made the wedding gown of a family member so very special.

The wedding slip of my Great-Great Aunt Mary was given to my Grandmother after my Mother was born. Grandmother designed and sewed my Mom's Baptismal gown from this heirloom treasure.

All five of my brothers and sisters were Christened in this gown, as well as my two daughters, and my first Granddaughter.

Generally, the bride did not carry a bouquet of flowers in her hands. Instead, it was tucked into the waistband of the wedding dress. Additionally, there was no throwing of the bouquet to any of the unmarried women attending the reception. Instead, the bride took her flowers home and dried them in the pages of the family Bible as a treasured remembrance of her special day.

The wedding toast was also very simple. The guests raised their glasses and toasted the happy couple with one word, *SLÁINTE*, (slancha), roughly translated as *health* or *cheers*.

CHAPTER SIXTEEN

♥

Neither Eliza nor Liam had the time or money to take the traditional wedding trip. It was planting season, and the fields needed to be prepared for the potato crop. Instead, the newlyweds returned to the Charlton cottage to spend the night. Katie had already packed her bag and was headed to Liam's family home to spend a few nights.

After only two nights away from home, Katie was looking forward to sleeping in her own loft again. As she approached the cottage, she saw Eliza and Liam working side-by-side in the fields. Eliza looked up and smiled when she heard her sister call out her name.

"*Céad mile fáilte* (cayd mala fall-cha), me dear!" Eliza hailed Katie with the traditional greeting of '*a hundred thousand welcomes.*'

Katie raced into the field and tightly hugged her sister. Then, she turned to Liam, hugged him, and again welcomed him into their family. Everyone was jovial and they even stopped their work in the field to share lunch with their newly-returned sister.

Following the blessing, Eliza was the first to initiate the conversation. "Sure, Katie me darling', we are so happy to have you home with us to celebrate Easter Sunday. Liam's entire family is joining us after Mass for a fun-filled celebration with all his nieces and nephews. I will surely need your help keeping all his young relatives amused. I am a wee bit nervous having such a large crowd for supper, especially since we were just married!"

"Dunna' worry!" Katie encouraged her sister. "You have already fed a large group many times before ... 'tis called our brothers and sisters!"

Katie hesitated before she continued to speak. "Dearest Eliza and Liam, I am truly sorry to tell you, but I already have plans for Easter Sunday, and I will not be here to help you."

Eliza tried to mask her disappointment, but her voice betrayed her emotions. "I sincerely hope that your plans do not include Mr. James Connolly." Suddenly Eliza's voice was dripping with distain. "If you plan on meeting this man, let me first tell you he is married and I will definitely not allow it!"

"Sure, I already know he is a married man!" Katie laughed. "His wife and meself are very good friends. And when they introduce me to everyone, I am always referred to as 'little sister.' For your information, Eliza, James and his wife helped me cope with my part in Da's death. I owe both so much for everything! Besides, James and his family are not here in Sligo, but have moved to Dublin with his volunteers."

"Where are you goin' to be on such a sacred and holy day?" Eliza continued to probe.

"I canna' tell you, Eliza! I have confidential knowledge of planned activities and I have sworn not to tell another living soul. Would you ever expect me to break a solemn oath?"

Eliza put her hands to her head in utter frustration. "What have you gotten yourself into, Katie? Are you in danger of being arrested?"

Katie saw the concern on her sister's face and tried to reassure her with her words. "Dunna' worry about me, dearest. I am just a baby fish swimmin' around in a big ocean. The British would never be interested in me. Additionally, our Irish army would never put me in harm's way. Every time I walk home from one of our meetings, I am never alone and I am always well protected."

"So, you are still sneaking off to attend secret meetings with plans for a revolution?"

Katie just nodded her head in the affirmative, and tried hard to think of a way to change the topic of conversation.

Meanwhile, Eliza had also arrived at her own realization that her sister was never going to break her word to the rebels and reveal their plans. Therefore, she stopped her questions and concentrated on enjoying her time with her sister.

The Irish language is not an easy language for the English-speaker to learn. It consists of two possible sounds for each consonant – the *broad sound* and the *slender sound*.

For example, the broad sound of the letter '**S**' is '*suh*,' while the slender sound is '*shuh*.'

The only way you can tell the difference between the broad and slender sound, is by looking at the vowels that flank the consonant. The *slender* consonant will be flanked by an '**I**' or an '**E**.' While the *broad* sound consonant will be flanked by either the letter '**A**,' '**O**' or the letter '**U**.'

This makes the Irish language very difficult to pronounce because each word contains many silent vowels whose only purpose is to signal the exact sound of a consonant.

James Connolly and his wife, Lilly, relocated to Dublin in preparation for the Easter Uprising of 1916. James had not yet shared that the plans formulated with the Germans for guns had been thwarted by the English. This seizure of weapons would put the Irish troops at a marked disadvantage against the heavily armed British forces.

CHAPTER SEVENTEEN

♥

On Easter Sunday, Eliza awoke before sunrise. She quietly climbed the ladder to the sleeping loft to check on Katie ... but her sister's sleeping mat was empty ... Katie was gone!

"Where could our little vixen have gone when the sun hasn't even peeked above tah horizon?" Eliza whispered to herself. Her voice was full of concern for her innocent sibling, and she prayed that Katie was out of harm's way.

Attempting to keep herself busy, Eliza quietly went about her morning chores careful not to wake Liam. He was working so hard to get the ground ready for planting, that he needed as much rest as possible. Thinking about her new husband made Eliza smile, and soon she found herself humming one of her favorite Easter hymns.

"*Jesus Christ is risen today! Alleluia*!"

Eliza was startled when Liam embraced her from behind and murmured into her ear, "What a wonderful Easter morn' to wake to me wife singin' in our kitchen!"

"I really shouldna' me happy, Liam," Eliza explained. "Me sister is already off on her secret mission and I dunna' know where she is or what she is doing!"

"Sure, Eliza, Katie is old enough to make her own decisions and know what is right for herself. Dunna' worry, me love! Let us enjoy our first Easter together. When we are finished with breakfast, I will even help clean our dishes and set out what we need for my family's visit."

Eliza smiled at her husband – she truly loved this simple farmer who had patiently waited for her to agree to marry him. Eliza was so grateful. Even though Katie was determined to leave Ireland, Liam would always be by her side. He loved the hard work on the farm, and had absolutely no desire to leave his homeland.

"Come, Eliza!" Liam's voice interrupted her deep thoughts. "Breakfast is ready and you must eat a little something before we head off to Church.

Eliza turned, and Liam saw the tears in her eyes. "Oh, me darlin,' why so sad on our church's glorious Holy Day? Are you truly worried about Katie's safety? We can always cancel our plans with my family, go into Sligo Town and look for her."

"Oh Liam, I am just a silly, over-protective sister who canna' bear to see Katie leave our home and head for America. My heart will be left with a huge hole once she is gone. I thank God I have you, me dear, to love me forever!"

Liam gently took his wife's hand to lend support and comfort. He didn't want to say anything to upset Eliza, but he knew that Katie would never be happy living in Ireland. America was calling her, and she was a free spirit who needed to pursue her dreams of guaranteed freedom.

Eliza dried her tears on her apron, and then made final preparations for Liam's family before leaving for Mass.

Everyone at their church was happy to greet the newlyweds. Some asked about Katie, but Eliza simply looked downward and shook her head. She could not answer for her sister's whereabouts, and was relieved when the bell tolled and the congregation moved inside to celebrate Mass.

After the service ended, Liam's family joined with Eliza and Liam for the walk back to the Charlton cottage. Then, the men carried benches outside for seating, and assembled make-shift tables for the food. Eliza had made several *Shepherd's Pies* for the main course, along with a fresh garden salad, and three different kinds of potatoes.

Everyone's spirits were high and laughter filled the air!

Attending Mass was always a religious and a social event for Catholics on the West Coast. It was a time to come together as a community – family and friends – to praise God. It was also a time to visit with their neighbors, discuss news-worthy events, and even share gossip!

In Ireland, beef was extremely expensive and was reserved for the wealthy landlords. The poor Irish celebrated with lamb, which was much less dear, and plentiful. (Even today, as you drive along the single-lane roads of the coast, you will have to yield the right-of-way to herds of sheep as they meander on the road!)

When you combine the availability of lamb with the potato crop, and the carrots and peas that thrive in Sligo's soil, you have all the ingredients for a delicious *Shepherds' Pie*.

Pubs in The United States tend to substitute ground beef for the lamb when preparing Shepherd's Pie, but it is still a very popular and delicious dish.

CHAPTER EIGHTEEN

♥

As the sun began to set, Liam's family said their goodbyes and headed for their homes.

Eliza took off her shoes and sat down in the lush green grass to try to relax. She was exhausted, but found that as hard as she tried, she was too tense and worried about Katie to relax. Liam sat down next to his wife, and pulled her head down on to his shoulder. After a few minutes, Liam suggested that it was time to go inside and prepare for bed.

"Oh, Liam, I canna' rest until Katie is home safely and asleep in our loft."

Liam shook his head. "You canna' wait all night for your sister's return. We dunna' even know if she will be back to our cottage before sunrise. Please, Eliza, come inside and try to rest."

Reluctantly, Eliza took Liam's extended hand and walked slowly toward the cottage. Before entering, she took one final look over her shoulder, just to see if there was a possibility that Katie would be exiting the woods toward home.

The next morning, Easter Monday, Katie had still not returned. It was not until very late that evening that Eliza heard her sister singing as she approached home.

Eliza jumped out of bed and ran to the front door just as her sister was about to enter. Katie laughed when she saw that Eliza was only dressed in her nightshirt. "And what would the neighbors think if they saw you outside in your nightshirt?" Katie teased.

Eliza stepped aside in order to let her sister enter the cottage first, then followed closely behind her. "Begorrah, Katie, where have you been for two whole days? I have been worried sick!"

"Sure, I have only been in Sligo Town, organizing, marching, and showing support for our Irish volunteers in Dublin. Our brave men and women have taken control of several important buildings right in tah heart of our capital city. News coming from Dublin is very slow, so we dunna' know how our men are faring, but Easter Monday, 1916, will go down in history as a great day. We are now one step closer to independence!"

Eliza looked very concerned. "Did anyone call *Garda* to come and break up your parade? Was anyone detained?"

Katie looked very puzzled. "Why would someone call Garda to come to our parade? We were very orderly and comported ourselves with dignity and pride."

"But Katie ... " Eliza attempted to continue her inquiry.

"Yes, Eliza, our local Garda was present along the side of the road." Katie interrupted. "No one was arrested and I dinna' see anyone writing down the names of our marchers. I am sure your home is safe, and no one will come in dead of night to drag me off to prison as a conspirator!"

"Do not make light of what you have done today!" Eliza scolded her sister. "First of all, our cottage does not belong to just Liam and meself. It is tah Charlton home and belongs to all of us. Secondly, Irish rebels have been dragged from homes during dark nights, with no witnesses, never to be seen again. I could never be happy if I knew you were sent to a penal colony in Australia – the other side of the world, Katie! You would be lost to me forever!"

"Now, Eliza," Katie began to speak very calmly, "let's not be so dramatic, please! I was never in any danger by marching in support of a free Ireland. I am just a simple country girl with no real power to change a small part of our world. 'Tis left to men like James Connolly, Patrick Pearse, and Thomas Clarke, to name just a few, who are the freedom fighters and will bring about change. Surely, all our men in Dublin face terrible danger and are willing to fight and die for our cause."

Immediately, Eliza knew that she would never win an argument with Katie when it came to the topic of independence for Ireland. She clearly saw that her nineteen-year-old sister was convinced that she would never face reprisal for her Easter week demonstration against the government. Katie was a stubborn Irishwoman, and she was never going to agree with her older sister.

Eliza quickly changed the topic from their controversial political beliefs to a more palatable topic of food. "Are you hungry, Katie? I have just made a pot of potato vegetable soup and it is still warm on the hearth. Please, help yourself, and dunna' forget to clean up!"

Katie stepped forward and hugged her thoughtful sister. She desperately wanted to reassure her that everything was alright. "Always remember, dear Eliza, I truly love you!"

As Katie turned toward the fireplace, she heard Eliza softly sob, and she felt an arrow of pain pierce her heart.

"Dear God, I know Eliza cares for me. Please hear my prayer and help her to understand why I must support the freedom fighters. Amen."

Garda is the name for the State Police Force in Ireland.

Today's Garda patrols without carrying any weapons. Most walk the beat, some ride bicycles, and the remainder cruise the streets in patrol cars. However, it should be noted, if a crisis situation arises, the officers can return to their precincts and retrieve their service guns.

The 1916 Irish Uprising or Rebellion, never really stood a chance of victory. The British had already seized the German shipment of guns that the rebels desperately needed to ensure their successful fight. Plus, the rebel's rationale that England was too heavily entrenched in fighting World War I to send troops, also proved to be grossly underestimated.

There were actually three rebel groups that came together for the uprising.

The first, *The Irish Republican Brotherhood* (IRB), was founded in the mid 1800's and was a secret organization comprised of anti-British revolutionaries. Sean McDermott. a high-ranking officer of this group, was the principle organizer of The Easter Uprising. His group was also known as the *Fenians*.

The second unit was *The Anti-War Volunteers*, a splinter group from Redmond's Volunteers of 1914. They were led by Éoin MacNeill, and they believed that it was wrong to wage an unprovoked attack against the British. MacNeill wanted his volunteers to wait until the English government began drafting Irish citizens to fight in WW I before they took action. The most important member of this group was the poet Patrick Pearse, who began his own Gaelic-speaking school in an effort to preserve the Irish language and traditions. Pearse openly wrote about his desire to be a martyr for the Irish cause. He was elected president of the very short-lived Republic that was established by the volunteers. Pierce became the face of the Irish Revolution.

The third group was *The Irish Volunteers* led by Thomas MacDonagh, A poet like Pearse, MacDonagh became the very first teacher to be employed by Saint Edna's School for Boys. He joined the Irish Volunteers in 1913, and then in 1915, became a member of the Irish Republican Brotherhood.

Four hundred and eighty-five individuals died during the week-long Easter Uprising, and more than two thousand were injured. Most injuries were recorded as the result of the indiscriminate firing by the English troops.

CHAPTER NINETEEN

♥

Over the course of the following week, Eliza kept a close watch over Katie. Every strange noise or knock on the door, caused Eliza's stomach to churn. She found it difficult to sleep, plus, her normal easy-going temperament was stretched way beyond its limit.

On the other hand, Katie was very calm as she anxiously awaited word from Dublin. She held to the notion that no news could indicate that the rebels had won and were busy establishing their own government. Katie did, however, stop every caravan of tinkers to seek any news they had from the capital city.

Finally, after more than two weeks, news of the rebellion trickled into Sligo. The newspapers reported that the rebels had held off the British soldiers for almost seven days before they made an unconditional surrender to the opposing side.

The Crown labeled all the Irish leaders as traitors and scheduled them for execution. On May 03, 1916, James Connolly, Patrick Pearse, Thomas Clarke, Sean MacDermott, Joseph Plunkett, and Thomas MacDonagh all faced the firing squad. Éamon de Valera, who was born in the United States, was not executed, but rather sentenced to prison.

It was British Commander Maxwell who carried out all the executions at Kilmainham Goal in Dublin. Then, the Commander ordered a country-wide search for anyone who had previous knowledge of the attempted coup. Arrests were made, and many individuals that had absolutely no involvement with the rebels were carted off to prison.

Katie fell to the ground, reduced to tears, after reading the reports published in the Dublin newspapers. She was still clutching the papers in her hand, when Liam helped her to stand and guided her toward the cottage. She never spoke one word, just buried her head in Liam's chest and sobbed.

Eliza's heart was breaking as she witnessed her sister's pain-filled cries. She hurried ahead to open the front door for Katie and her husband to enter.

As they passed over the threshold, Eliza saw the papers that were still grasped in Katie's hand. She gently removed them, and once safely inside the house, began to read the reports. As Eliza read, she realized that it would not take long for the soldiers to find Katie and arrest her. Stunned, she raced into her bedroom and pulled the only suitcase they owned from under the bed. Then, she began packing clothes for Katie.

When Liam entered the bedroom, he was shocked to see his wife wildly tossing clothes into the battered suitcase.

"Eliza, me darlin', whatever are you doing?" He questioned his highly agitated spouse.

Eliza simply handed Liam the newspaper clippings and closely watched his face as he slowly digested the news.

"I will head into Sligo tonight and check when our next ship is bound for America. Eliza, you keep packing, but try to keep her suitcase light since Katie will have to carry it herself. I will book passage for her as soon as room is available onboard. I will return as quickly as possible."

Liam hugged Eliza as he headed to the barn to saddle his horse.

After Eliza completed the packing, she climbed the ladder to the sleeping loft to check on her sister. Katie had stopped crying, however, she appeared dazed as she looked up at the thatched roof with a blank expression on her face.

"Katie," Eliza whispered, "can we talk?"

Katie just shook her head in the affirmative and continued with her blank stare.

"Liam has ridden into town to book passage for you to America. We must move very quickly since British forces are combing our countryside looking to arrest anyone who had knowledge of Connolly's rebellion. You must leave Ireland, me darlin', as soon as possible. I have already packed a bag for you, so you will be able to leave as soon as Liam returns with news.

Katie sat up straight on her sleeping mat. "Are you and Liam coming with me to America?"

"No, me darlin', our life and farm are here and we will be happy together in Sligo. You have friends in New York who already have a place for you. You will be safe with Nora and Marion's families in Buffalo."

Eliza reached out and clutched Katie against her breast. She wondered if her youngest sister could hear the sound of her heart breaking in two? Eliza's eyes flooded over with tears as the understanding of Katie's imminent departure was about to become a reality. Due to her sister's well-known friendship and strong ties to James Connolly and his wife, she was being forced to leave her beloved homeland.

"I am so sorry, Eliza!" Katie cried. "I never wanted to leave Ireland under terrifying conditions. I always wanted me parting to be a happy occasion where I would wave a white handkerchief from the top deck of my ship to all my loved ones on tah dock. Instead, I will have to sneak aboard me departing ship and hope no one will recognize me as a friend to rebels. I am so very sorry, me dear Eliza!"

Soon the sisters heard the sound of Liam's old horse galloping into the yard. He tied his exhausted mare and rushed into the cottage, anxious to share his news.

"A ship is leaving tomorrow morning for America from Salthill, Galway. But we must leave now so that we can make its early morning departure. Unfortunately, I was only able to book passage in steerage – 'tis not a pleasant place to stay, but I know you will make tah best of it, Katie. Now, however, I must go and hitch my wagon so both of us can leave as soon as possible. Please say your goodbyes while I am in our barn."

Katie reached into her deep pocket and handed Eliza a large envelope filled with the money she had earned from the sale of her lace. "Here, Eliza, give this to Liam in order to repay for me ticket abroad."

Eliza shook her head. "No, me dear. You will need all your money when you land in New York. Liam and meself are happy to use our wedding gifts to pay your way and make sure you are safe."

"How can I ever reimburse you for all you and Liam have done for me? Will you ride with us to Salthill so we can say a proper farewell before I board my ship?"

"I am afraid I could put you in danger if the house is empty when British soldiers come. It would look very suspicious, and troops would begin to search for you. If I am here, I will say you and Liam are taking vegetables to market for sale. I am sure I can sound very believable!"

Katie took two steps toward Eliza and opened her arms for one final embrace. Eliza slowly recited the old Irish blessing into Katie's ear:

> *May the road rise up to meet you,*
> *May the wind be always at your back,*
> *May the sun shine warm upon your face,*
> *The rain fall soft upon your fields,*
> *And until we meet again,*
> *May God hold you in the hollow of His hand."*

Then, Eliza kissed Katie one final time and walked with her to the door.

After the wagon was underway, Katie turned one final time to wave goodbye to her beloved sister. There was Eliza, standing outside the doorway and waving a white handkerchief as the wagon rode out of sight.

Éamon de Valera was born on October 14, 1882, in Manhattan, New York, to an Irish mother and a Spanish father. As a toddler, he was sent to live in Limerick with his mother's family.

Later, during his college years, de Valera developed a strong hatred of the British and their harsh rule of the Irish population. In November, 1913, he joined the Irish Volunteers, and in 1916, he was elected second in command during the Easter Uprising. Due to the fact that he was an American citizen, he was sentenced to a prison term instead of execution.

After two years in prison, de Valera was released and represented the Sinn Féin party in the general election. He also returned to The United States in 1919 to solicit funds for the freedom movement.

Éamon was elected President of Southern Ireland in 1959, and continued to serve in that capacity until 1973. He died just two years after his retirement at 92 years of age. President de Valera is one of the outstanding heroes in Irish history – securing total freedom for 23 of the 32 Irish counties.

As an aside, Eliza had raised my Grandmother since infancy, and always looked upon her as one of her own children. Unfortunately, Eliza and Liam never had children of their own; however, Eliza communicated with Katie regularly through 'snail mail,' and the two sisters never let distance effect their love. It was a very sad day in our home in Buffalo, New York, when my Grandmother received word that Eliza had passed.

CHAPTER TWENTY

♥

As Katie approached the ocean liner, it looked huge and extremely frightening. Liam walked up the gangway behind Katie, carrying her suitcase and a small container of food for her breakfast. Katie, however, handed the food back to Liam, explaining that she was too nervous to eat, so the food would only go to waste.

Liam smiled at his new sister-in-law and drew her aside to say his farewell. "Katie, dunna' forget us when you reach America. We will look forward to your letters whenever you can write. Remember, Ireland is your home, and you will always be welcomed back by your family and friends. God bless you, me darlin' Katie, and God's speed!"

A quick kiss on Katie's cheek, and Liam was gone. She felt overwhelmed and lonely at the thought of traveling across the Atlantic Ocean by herself. Katie decided to follow the advice that her Dad always gave to her when she was down ... "*pull yourself up by your bootstraps, me girl, and only go forward!*" And that was exactly what she was going to do. James Connolly and his volunteers did not give up their lives in vain! "I am goin' to devote me life to helping others in their name!"

Meanwhile, the ship's bursar had been watching the striking young woman standing alone on the deck. Finally, he approached her. "Miss, may I help you to locate your cabin?"

Katie shook her head. "I have no cabin, sir. I am to travel to New York below in steerage."

"I am so sorry." The handsome bursar replied. "It is not the most pleasant way to travel. If I had an extra bed available, I would move you to one of the deck rooms, but the ship is full to capacity. The war in Europe has caused so many of the people to escape the violence by seeking refuge in America."

The bursar sounded so sad that Katie felt compelled to smile and reassure him. "My name is Katie Charlton and I am truly moved by your kindness, sir."

"And my name is Patrick O'Hara from New York City. I am pleased to make your acquaintance."

"I am happy to meet you too, Patrick! I am headed for New York, as well, and my second stop is a city called Buffalo. I have friends there who will help me settle into my new life.

Patrick gave a slight bow. "You are definitely Irish, Katie, for I can tell by your strong brogue. My grandfather came from County Cork years ago to escape …"

Patrick quickly stopped speaking and looked at his supervisor. "I must get back to work right away, but I will try to find you when they allow steerage passengers up on deck for fresh air. Goodbye for now, Katie Charlton!"

Katie had no idea what awaited her as she descended the stairway into steerage. Men, women and children were all huddled together and some appeared to be in a state of shock! Katie smiled at everyone she passed in her search for a quiet place to claim as her own. The sight below deck was terrifying. There was crying, others were coughing, while others closed their eyes and prayed. The next five days would prove to be a challenge for the wary nineteen-year-old.

Katie soon discovered that it was impossible for her to sleep that first night. Many of the children were seasick and their mothers were unable to soothe them. Their cries tugged at Katie's heartstrings, so she climbed off her thin mattress and volunteered to help wherever she was needed. She spent half the night walking the floor carrying a crying baby in her arms, carefully avoiding all personal spaces as she navigated through the tight living quarters. Everyone was so grateful for her assistance and quickly befriended her.

Just as the sun broke the horizon, Katie collapsed on her mattress and closed her eyes. Suddenly, a loud voice blasted into the cramped quarters. "All those wishing to partake of breakfast, please come to the main deck. You will be allowed to wash up and then walk around deck after your morning ablutions."

Katie turned to the young woman next to her. "Sure, I believed it was God's voice calling out to me when I opened me eyes!" Katie laughed. "And hello to you! Me name is Katie Charlton from County Sligo." She announced as she extended her hand in friendship.

"My name is Anna Grant from Liverpool, England. I am happy to make your acquaintance." Anna smiled at her new friend. "I hope you will not hold it against me that I am English and you are Irish. I am not into politics and I like everyone!"

"Soon, we will both be living in America, so I dunna' believe it really matters." Katie responded with a huge grin on her tired face.

"Where are you headed Katie, my new friend with the beautiful auburn hair." Anna inquired.

"I plan to make my way to a city called Buffalo, in New York State. I have my two best friends waitin' for me to arrive. I already have a job, as well as a place to live."

Anna smiled. "I will be near Buffalo, Katie. I will live in a growing city called Rochester. Although not as big as Buffalo, all my family is living there and have already secured a job for me. I will be the last family member to arrive in America. For some reason, I had difficulty with my paperwork and had to wait almost three extra months for the government to work out the details."

"Paperwork!" Katie cried. "What paperwork do we need to land at Ellis Island?"

Anna could see that her new friend was about to cry. "If your paperwork isn't in order, Katie, I can give you some helpful hints on what you can do to enter America. Although some of my family didn't have the proper paperwork, we were still able to get them into the country. Some here as classed as *illegal aliens*; however, the government never bothers them. They get jobs and settle down to a quiet life.

All the color drained from Katie's face and her eyes brimmed with tears. "Illegal means that I would be breakin' the law, and Anna, I canna' go to jail. I had to leave Ireland very quickly because British soldiers were arresting anyone who had contact with Irish rebels. I was friends with one leader and his wife. When my sister, Eliza, discovered I was about to be arrested, she had her husband drive me in dead of night to another town so no one could find me. I dunna' have any papers, Anna! Whatever am I to do?"

"Do not worry, Katie. I will tell you all the different ways that my family crossed into The United States. I will even explain all about their contingency plans tonight after most have settled down and are asleep."

"If anyone actually gets to sleep tonight!" Katie joked. "God willing, the babies will be so tired after last night, all will sleep soundly. Perhaps the only one awake will be me because I am so scared about my future!"

Anna stood, grabbed Katie's arm, and headed up to the main deck. Anna seemed very upset when she discovered that breakfast consisted of a hard roll and a cup of milk.

Katie, on the other hand, was thankful for all the food offered, and after saying her silent prayer of gratitude, never complained as she took her first bite.

"Have you ever tasted Irish butter?" Katie asked as they walked around deck. "It is so rich and so sweet. You will never want anything else on your roll! I will truly miss Eliza's home churned butter!"

"As for me," Anna continued her complaint, "I would love for someone to offer me a cup of coffee. I find that I never really have any energy until I sit down with my morning coffee!"

Suddenly, Katie stopped walking when she heard her name called out from behind her. When she turned, she discovered Patrick, the bursar, carrying a large cloth-covered tray.

"Let us find a quiet place to sit." Patrick suggested. "Katie, I have brought breakfast for you and your friend."

Anna found the perfect spot next to one of the lifeboats, and it was even shaded from the sun, so they could sit and eat in comfort.

"I brought a pot of coffee, as well as a pot of tea, because I didn't know which one you would prefer. There are also some pastries, scrambled eggs, and a large slice of ham."

"Coffee!" Anna shrieked. "That is all I really need to make my day! Patrick, you are my hero!"

Katie laughed as she sipped her hot tea. "Sure, Patrick, you are me hero too. Such a thoughtful gift for two weary travelers who were not able to catch a wink of sleep last night."

"Was it too hot below deck for you?" Patrick inquired. "I was worried that the heat would be stifling and breathing would be difficult."

"No, it was not the heat." Katie related as she took a bite of her pastry. "Steerage feels all movement of waves, and 'twas hard for the babes aboard. Poor darlin's were sick and crying. I am sure all will be better tonight. One new mum is having difficulty feeding her baby. Do you mind if we share some of our food so she will be strong enough to nurse her wee one?"

Patrick smiled down at Katie. "Show me where she is, and I will bring her over for something to eat."

Anna and Katie perused the deck until they located the young mother. Anna pointed her out to Patrick. "Over there, by the railing. She is the one with the brown shawl wrapped around the babe."

Patrick quickly brought the young mother over to the lifeboat and held the baby while she sat and ate her breakfast.

"How kind you all are," she gushed as she ate the scrambled eggs. "I am very weak and not producing enough milk for little Jeremy. Now, I feel so much better, and even the tea has settled my stomach. I cannot thank you enough."

Katie wrapped the slice of ham in a napkin and handed it to the new mom. "Just something for you to snack on later and keep your energy level up."

Patrick carefully handed the baby back to his mom. "I can let the ship's doctor know about your condition. Then, he can lend a hand if things do not get better for you."

"Thank you so very much! My name is Margaret Ford and I am from London, England. My husband is in The United States Army and has been ordered back home to Virginia. Jeremy and I are going to join him there. "Then, she kissed Patrick on the cheek, waved goodbye to her two new friends, and was quickly away.

Katie stood up on tiptoe and also kissed Patrick's cheek. "Your kindness has fed three people today, Patrick. I canna' tell you what it means to me. I am so happy we met yesterday as I stood alone and confused on deck. You, young man, are a kindred spirit!"

Patrick blushed a bright shade of pink as he bent down to retrieve the tray from the deck. "I must be off to work. Remember to stop by the fresh water buckets that are placed around deck so that you can refresh yourself for the day. One of the stewards will empty the bucket when you are finished. Then, continue on your walk until the whistle blows to signal your time on deck is complete. I will try to see you again for breakfast tomorrow morning."

Anna stood and slid her arm into the crook of Katie's elbow as they continued to walk. "You make pretty impressive friends in high places, my dear! I never thought we would be having breakfast with such a handsome young man!"

"Come now, Anna, and stop your silly talk. We still have much to do before the whistle blows."

The girls had just finished washing up when the whistle sounded and they headed for the steerage stairway. As they descended, they realized that it didn't seem as bleak now that they were refreshed. The passengers were busy stringing up blankets and sheets for more privacy. Katie and Anna pitched right in and helped the men, while the women entertained the children. After a light evening meal, everyone settled down in the semi-darkness and all was very quiet.

Anna moved closer to Katie's mattress and whispered, "Katie, are you ready to talk? I want to help you make plans for when we meet the Inspectors at Ellis Island. I do not want you to fret, but you do need to be ready for all their questions."

"I dunna' believe I will be doing much talking before police cart me off to jail as an illegal!"

Katie was shocked when she heard Anna giggle at her dilemma!

"I am so sorry I laughed at your difficulty!" Anna apologized. "You will not be dragged off to jail by the police, Katie. They will not even let you leave the boat if they suspect your papers are not in order. Instead, they will send you up north to Toronto, Canada, where you will be welcomed by their government. Once docked there, the officers will let you off the boat. Please, do not be afraid, Katie! There is a bridge over the Niagara River joining The United States with Canada. They call it *The Honeymoon Bridge* – isn't that a wonderful, romantic name? That is where the bus will cross over to New York. All you need to know for the Canadian government is your name, birthdate and year, plus your country of origin."

"Oh, Anna!" Katie moaned. "Sure, it will be hard for you to understand, but I dunna' know when I was born. I remember me Mum telling me it was in springtime because Da had been out working in our fields, but I dunna' have any more details."

Anna looked puzzled. "Surely you must know when your birthday is?"

"We never celebrated our birthdays." Katie whispered. "With seven children, my parents couldna' afford any celebrations. And now I am doomed to never see my friends in America!"

"Now wait," Anna interrupted. You look to be about the same age as me, so let's say that you were born in 1891. Next, let's pick a birth month. Your Mum told you that you arrived in the springtime, so tell me what month you would like to pick."

Finally, Katie smiled. "I want the seventeenth day of March as my birthday. Sure, 'tis the feast day for Saint Patrick, our patron saint of Ireland. He was a very holy man who drove all the snakes out of Ireland and brought us Christianity. Saint Patrick used our beloved shamrock to teach us all about the Holy Trinity. I would be so honored to share his feast day."

"Then it is settled!" Anna proclaimed. "Katie Charlton of Sligo County, Ireland, was born on the seventeenth day of March in the year 1891. Now, how does that new identity make you feel?"

"I feel happy again, dear Anna! I am not afraid because eventually I will have Canadian documents to enter my new homeland!"

Anna was thankful that Katie could not see her face clearly in the semi-darkness. How was she going to explain that the Canadian papers would only allow her to visit her friends in The United States? Ultimately, Katie would have to return to Canada, submit the proper paperwork for legal entry into the US, which could take years to process. Quickly, Anna came to the conclusion that she would not burden her friend with all the complicated details.

In 1916, the Immigration Laws of The United States clearly stated three important requirements for entry into the country.

First, you had to have a sponsor, an individual who was a US citizen, and ready to assume all financial responsibility for you.

Second, you must already have a place to live – a residence with a mailing address. This was usually provided by your sponsor.

And, third, you must prove that full-time employment is guaranteed. You would not be allowed to enter the US through Ellis Island without meeting these basic requirements.

In the beginning of the 20th century, Irish immigrants flooded into the US. Signs appeared in shop windows announcing, *'Irish need not apply!'* It became extremely impossible for the Irish to secure employment, except in the fields of law enforcement, city fire departments, or sanitation positions.

As a child, I was told the story that Saint Patrick drove all the snakes out of Ireland. Archeologists and historians report that there had not been snakes in Ireland prior to the first ice age. However, in Biblical times, the snake always represented evil; for example, the snake tempting Eve with the apple in the Garden of Eden. (However, similar to Greenland's and Alaska's weather and isolation, they too do not have any snakes!)

Legend says that Saint Patrick banged his staff three times on the ground, and all the frightened snakes quickly deserted Ireland. This supposed *miracle* did increase Patrick's popularity in Ireland.

Another interesting fact pertinent to my Grandmother's arrival in the US, is that her bus that departed from Toronto, would have entered this country using the *Honeymoon Bridge* which spanned the Niagara River Gorge shared by The United States and Canada. The bridge received its name due to the fact that Niagara Falls was always considered the honeymoon capital of the world.

In 1938, the Honeymoon Bridge collapsed into the gorge due to the severe ice buildup at the base of the bridge. The famous Peace Bridge, still in use today, did not open until 1927.

CHAPTER TWENTY-ONE

♥

Katie and Anna were both on deck when The Statue of Liberty came into view as the ship entered New York Harbor. Katie felt tears build behind her eyes as she realized that she had traveled so far, and was so close to freedom; however, it was highly unlikely she would set foot on US soil. Anna, respecting Katie's plight, restrained herself from exhibiting her enthusiasm over her arrival.

Unexpectedly, Patrick tapped Katie on her shoulder. When she turned, Patrick smiled and handed her a small white envelope. "It is my address and phone number in New York City." He explained. "I live with my parents, so there is always someone there to take a message for me. If you ever need help, please call. I am state-side for the next week; then, I am back to sea for ten days."

Katie smiled at the handsome young man. "Oh, Patrick, I wish all was well, but I am afraid I am bound for Canada because I dunna' have proper paperwork to enter your country."

"Telephones still work in Canada, my dear Katie." Patrick explained. "You can always call me collect so that you don't have to pay anything for the call."

Knowing nothing about the workings of a telephone, Katie just smiled and tucked Patrick's note into her pocket. "I am so happy I met you, dear Patrick! Your friendship, all the extra food, and making meself feel more comfortable when I came aboard, all show what a true friend you are." Katie threw her arms around his neck and kissed his cheek.

Anna was next in line to add another kiss to Patrick's cheek and thank him for his kindness. Poor Patrick was red-faced from all the attention bestowed on him from the girls. He finally waved goodbye and disappeared into the gathering crowd.

First-class passengers disembarked first. They would be processed very quickly through Ellis Island's processing center. Second-class passengers were next in line, and they required more time to be cleared for entry. Finally, the steerage arrivals would be the last to be processed.

Immigration Officers would come aboard the ship and check for the proper paperwork before allowing anyone from steerage to leave the ship and progress to the next stage of entry.

Anna kissed Katie's cheek and told her that they would surely meet again. After all, Anna believed that New York State couldn't be that large!

Once again, Katie found herself completely alone. As she stood on deck, an

Immigration Inspector approached with a very stern face that frightened her.

"I am Katie Charlton form Sligo, Ireland, and I have learned I am without proper paperwork for entry."

The Inspector appeared quite surprised by the young lady's honesty. "W-well," he stammered, "I must send you off to Toronto, Canada, where the government will welcome you with open arms. I am sad to see such a polite young woman, like yourself, leave us, but our laws are very strict and very specific. Best of luck to you, Miss."

"And God bless you, Sir!" Katie replied before turning back on the deck.

After several hours of waiting, Katie felt the ship pull away from Ellis Island. She waved a white handkerchief from the upper deck railing with the hope that Anna would be looking up as they departed the harbor. Katie watched as hundreds and hundreds of individuals and families waited in line to be admitted into The United States of America, but sadly, Katie was not one of them.

From 1892 until 1954, Ellis Island was our nation's busiest immigrant processing station. During this time, the officers admitted more than twelve million individuals.

An immigrant with the proper paperwork, and classified as healthy by the attending physician, could expect to spend up to five hours waiting in line. A brief physical separated the sick individuals, and sent them to isolation in a hospital that had been erected on the Island.

Ellis Island earned the title *'Island of Tears,'* even though only two percent of the applicants were refused entry. Unfortunately, that number included my Grandmother!

Between 1920 and 1924, immigration reached an all-time high. *The National Origins Act* and *Quota Laws of 1924* were quickly passed. These laws were an attempt to control the newly arriving immigrants, who were considered inferior to the old immigrants of earlier times.

In November, 1954, Ellis Island was officially closed.

Today, Ellis Island is federally owned, and contains the records of those immigrants that entered through its gateway. Now, a museum, I was able to research my Grandfather, John Conlon's, arrival at Ellis Island. I was also able to retrieve his actual signature on the ship's manifest, the name of the ship, and the date of his arrival.

A mostly unknown fact that I learned at the Pierce Arrow Museum in Buffalo, New York, is that all the new immigrants processed through Ellis Island were given a box of Jell-O, invented by Mary Wait and Rose Knox. The owners used a horse-drawn *'Jell-O Wagon'* to distribute their welcome gifts to the new arrivals. This wagon, buried for years beneath junk in a mid-state barn, was recently discovered by the stars of the television show *The American Pickers*, and is displayed exactly as found, in the Pierce Arrow Museum in downtown Buffalo.

Also, this fact helps to explain why Jell-O was always a part of our holiday meals. Whether it was filled with fruit, or creamed with a thick whipped sauce, it was always part of our family celebrations. Now, I finally understand its significance!

CHAPTER TWENTY-TWO

♥

It was a hot summer night when Katie's ship arrived in Toronto, Canada. She stood up on deck taking in all the sights as they pulled into port.

Katie had never seen gas lamps before, and the dock was flooded with their light. Additionally, the summer heat was overpowering, and she found herself a bit dizzy, so she sat down on the deck next to a lifeboat.

It was from this vantage point that Katie noticed the dark-skinned, half-naked men working on the docks. She was certain that the ship had taken her to hell. Frightened, Katie climbed under the lifeboat and curled up in a ball.

Canadian Authorities were unable to reason with the young woman, so they called the bursar, who had befriended Katie, to come and try to talk some sense into his hysterical friend.

"Katie!" Patrick called under the lifeboat. "It is me, Patrick, and I would like you to come out so that I can talk to you."

Katie poked her head out to see her friend. "Oh Patrick, why are you here in hell with me? You are such a good person and so kind, God would never condemn you to hell for all eternity."

Patrick tried not to laugh. "And what makes you think that you are in hell, Katie? Please, tell me so I can understand."

Katie took a deep breath before she began to speak. "Sure, 'tis so very hot and I am surrounded by fire all around me. And men slaving away on tah dock have all had their skin burned by hell's fire!"

Patrick turned to the two Immigration Officers. "I think I can solve this problem if you just give me a few minutes to calm her down. Katie is from the west coast of Ireland, very superstitious, and has never seen gas lamps, black stevedores, or experienced heat from a summer's night."

The officers laughed and stepped away from the scene.

"Oh Katie, please come out and talk to me." Patrick pleaded. "The officials have backed away and are allowing me to speak with you and reassure you that you are safe. Please, come out!"

Katie slowly crawled from under the raft. "Do you feel I am just a big baby hiding meself away from all me fears?"

"No, not at all, my dear!" Patrick tried to console his friend. "I just need to explain a few of the things that have frightened you. Do you think that you are calm enough to listen to what I have to say?"

Katie shook her head in the affirmative.

"Well, first, it is summer here in Canada. The temperature gets very warm, even hot to someone like you. This alone, is one thing that you have never had to deal with before now. The men take off their shirts because it is easier for them to work without sweaty clothing sticking to their skin." Patrick explained. "And their skin has always been black – they were born that way, Katie. They are no different from you or me, just the color of their skin. And lastly, the gas lamps that seem to be lit with hell's fire – they are lit just as your candles at home are lit. There is a man who comes around just before darkness falls and lights each lamp with a special taper. We call him the old lamp lighter."

Finally, Katie smiled. Is he really old, Patrick?"

"I don't think so, but they probably think it is more romantic to sing about an old lamp lighter, rather than a rambunctious young boy!" Patrick teased.

"Now, Katie, we have something very important to talk about. The Immigration Officers are waiting to process you so that you can leave the ship. I have asked them to expedite your case so that you can visit your friends in Buffalo. They have also promised to escort you to a women's boarding house where you can spend the night safely. I must return to New York, so I cannot stay and help you."

"Oh Patrick! You have already done so much for me. I do feel a little foolish because I hid under a lifeboat, but you have helped me to see I dunna' have any reason to be afraid." Once, again, Katie stepped forward and kissed Patrick on his cheek. "Goodbye, my special friend!"

Patrick signaled the officers that they could approach. "She is ready to speak with you now. I have explained that you will also take her to the women's boarding house, so she understands that you are here to help her and not send her back to Ireland."

The first officer asked Katie if she had any questions before the interview began. Katie stood tall and proud as she indicated that she was definitely ready.

"Miss Charlton, can you please state your full name for me."

"Catherine Charlton, but I prefer to be called Katie."

"Very good, Katie. Now, can you tell us where and when you were born?'

"My home is County Sligo, Kilmacowen Parish, our land is called Carrowgabbadagh. I was born on tah seventeenth day of March in 1891 during spring planting."

The officer smiled. "You are giving us very detailed information, Katie. Now, why did you leave Ireland?"

Katie paused for a few seconds and seemed quite puzzled. "I probably should start at the beginning of my friendship with Mister James Connolly and his wife. They helped me adjust after the death of me Da."

"May I interrupt for one moment?" The second officer requested. Katie shook her head indicating that he should continue.

"Does the word 'Da' refer to your father?"

"Yes, sir."

"And the man you refer to as James Connolly, is he the rebel who led the recent Irish Uprising?"

"Yes, sir."

The officer smiled and told Katie to continue.

"Well, sir, about a week after James and all other leaders of our revolt were executed, British soldiers began rounding up anyone who had any association with James Connolly. All were carted off to jail. My sister, Eliza, believed I was in terrible danger because British authorities had seen me many times with James and his family. So, Eliza, and her new husband, Liam, packed me bag and I 'twas taken to Salthill, Galway, to escape capture."

"That is quite a story, Katie. In summary, you left Ireland and your family because you feared you would be arrested and jailed because of your association with James Connolly, one of the leaders of the Easter Rebellion. Is that correct?"

Frightened, Katie's voice shook when she replied. "Yes, sir."

Suddenly Katie was afraid that the Canadian Authorities would turn her over to the British Police.

"Miss Catherine Charlton from County Sligo, Kilmacowen Parish in Carrowgabbadagh, you have been declared an applicant for political asylum by Canadian Immigration. You will be issued temporary papers immediately. You can use these official documents to travel freely, even visiting your friends across the border in New York State."

Katie's eyes filled with tears. "Oh, you are wonderful men! I will never forget you and your kindness!"

Then, the two Immigration Officers escorted her down to the dock, presented her with her temporary papers, and walked her to the women's boarding house.

Katie was on her way to a good night's sleep and then on to Buffalo, New York!

Although hard to believe, my Grandmother did refuse to leave the ship when it docked in Toronto. The reasons were exactly as explained in this chapter.

In the early 1900's, the west coast of Ireland was fairly isolated. They did not have train service like the other parts of the Island, and they did not have any industry that would draw the attention of the British Crown. Sligo consisted of small, thatched-roof cottages that were handed down from generation to generation. Outhouses and chamber pots were the norm, and most houses only had outdoor water pumps to meet their needs.

Additionally, the weather in Ireland should be comparable to the weather conditions found in Greenland. However, the North Atlantic Current, which flows up the east coast of The United States, saves Ireland from becoming a frozen wasteland. When you consider that 3/4th of Greenland is covered by a permanent ice sheet, the winter temperatures in Ireland appear to be very mild. The average winter temperatures range from 46 to 49 degrees Fahrenheit. Summer temperatures have an average high of only 60 to 62 degrees on the coast. Therefore, for Katie to arrive in Canada on a hot summer night, where the temperature could still be above 80 degrees, would be very oppressive.

Lastly, this was the first time that my Grandmother had ever seen a black man. Now, perhaps, you can understand why she was afraid to disembark from the ship!

CHAPTER TWENTY-THREE

♥

The following morning, Katie was up with the sun. She ate a light breakfast, placed two apples in her pocket, and headed for the bus station.

It was another hot day in Toronto, and Katie was very glad that she had dressed in her lightest weight clothing. She ambled through the city, looking up at the two-story buildings, and then down at all the people walking the sidewalks. This was a new concept for Katie ... not having to walk in dirt roadways and avoid all the animal droppings. Sidewalks were her new delight and she couldn't wait to send Eliza the news in her next letter.

Katie followed the map that the Immigration Officer had drawn for her, and clutched it tightly in her hand. She could not afford to get lost in a strange city! When she arrived at the train station, Katie went straight to the first ticket booth and asked for a bus ticket to Buffalo, New York.

The ticket seller looked suspiciously at her worn clothing. "Do you have the money to pay for the ticket, Miss?"

Katie reached down into her pocket and pulled out a handful of Irish pound notes. "Oh, quickly child, put the money out of sight! You cannot afford to have someone steal your pound notes."

Katie did as she was told. "We have to exchange some of your Irish money into Canadian and American money." The ticket seller suggested.

Katie looked terribly confused. "In Ireland we only have one money system. Why would I ever need two different kinds of money?"

"Well, Miss, so many people assume that Canada is part of the US, but it is not. Canada is its own country with its own system of government and money. We may be tied to the British Crown, but we are our own people."

"My goodness, sir, I did not mean to upset you. Indeed, I know Canada is not part of America for they refused to let me in, but the Canadian Authorities welcomed me!"

The older man smiled and seemed to understand Katie's plight. "Now, the next bus for Buffalo does not leave for almost two hours. You have plenty of time to walk up the street to the Bank of Canada and exchange some of your money. Your bus ticket to Buffalo, New York will cost you twelve dollars Canadian."

Katie thanked the helpful man and headed down the street to the bank building. When she returned to the terminal, she walked right up to the same ticket booth.

"Here is my twelve dollars Canadian, sir."

"And here is your ticket into the US. Do you have the proper paperwork to enter at the

Immigration Border Crossing? I would hate to see you turned away after purchasing a ticket."

Once again, Katie reached into her oversized pocket and pulled out her documents. The man carefully looked over the official papers.

"These are temporary papers, Miss, so you must return within ten days to be given your permanent papers. You do understand the word temporary?"

"Yes, sir!" Katie responded. "I am just goin' fer-tah visit my two best friends from Ireland."

"Well, be on your way, dearie!" He advised. "And don't forget to have fun!"

Slowly, Katie walked through the station. She couldn't believe all the noise that surrounded her – people laughing, talking, and a loud speaker making announcements – all overwhelming for the simple country girl. When she climbed the steps of her bus, Katie didn't know where she was supposed to sit. She looked at the driver for help. "Sir, I have never been on a bus before and I do not know what I should do or where I should sit. Can you please help me?"

The young driver smiled. "Of course I can help you, young lady. Sit here in the front of the bus. The front window is very large and you will get a better view of the sights as we ride along. If you have any questions, just aske me, Jake Campbell, and I will give you the answer."

"I am Katie, and I have just one question. How long will it take to get to Buffalo?"

"That is not an easy question to answer. The roads are narrow, so if there is an accident, it could add hours on to a trip that usually takes me four to five hours to drive."

Katie sat down in the first seat, pulled one of her apples from her pocket and settled back to enjoy her first bus ride.

The view of all the farmland was beautiful, but the bus was crowded and very warm. Soon she found herself dropping off to sleep. That was when the driver announced over the intercom system that they were entering the US Immigration Plaza, and that everyone should have their paperwork ready for inspection. Katie was very nervous. After all, she was sitting in the first seat and would be the very first person checked by the authorities.

Officers entered the bus and politely asked to see her papers. Katie quickly complied, and her hands shook as she held out the papers. It seemed as if the inspection took forever, when actually it took only seconds.

"Very good, Miss Charlton, and welcome to The United States for your first visit."

Katie smiled at the driver who was watching her in the rearview mirror. "I canna' believe how easy it is to enter on land instead of trying to come ashore from a ship at Ellis Island."

Soon, the bus was back on the road headed to the train station in Buffalo. One of the passengers told Katie that since there was no real bus station, their bus would be arriving at the *Buffalo Central Terminal* that was being utilized even while it was currently under construction.

Once again, when she left the bus, Katie was faced with masses of people all rushing in different directions. She finally found a park bench and sat down to try and figure out what she should do next.

Suddenly, a police officer caught her attention, and she instantly knew that he would be the one to help her find her way.

"Excuse me, Officer," Katie began, "I am very lost and dunna' know how to get to the south side of Buffalo. Could you possibly help me, please?"

The officer smiled. "Sounds like you just got off the boat from Ireland, my dear, and I will be more than happy to help you." He was totally taken aback by the young lady's bright smile and dancing brown eyes. "Do you happen to have an address where you need to go?"

Katie reached into her bag and pulled out one of Nora's letters. She had forgotten that she had placed Marion's lucky stone inside the envelope to ensure that she returned it after all these years. Katie's face was horror-stricken as she watched the lucky stone fall to the ground and roll away.

The officer stretched out his shoe and stopped the stone from disappearing into the tall grass. "This must be a very important rock!" He teased.

Katie dropped the lucky stone back into her pocket. She had no intention of sharing her superstition with a complete stranger.

"If you follow me, Miss, I will take you to the precinct house and will make sure you reach your destination."

"You are so kind, sir. I hope someday I can return a favor for you."

"Well, my name is John Conlon and I live in South Buffalo, only two streets from the address on your envelope."

Katie stopped dead in her tracks. "John Conlon from Tobercurry, Ireland? The same John Conlon with an older brother named Paddy, who is our best fiddler in all of Sligo County?"

John laughed as he interrupted the inquisitive young woman. "One question at a time, please! I am originally from Tobercurry, and my brother is indeed Paddy, the gifted fiddler. How would you even know all this unless you were a neighbor to the Conlon's?"

Beggin' your pardon, John," Katie apologized. "I am Katie Charlton from Kilmacowen Parish in Sligo. I have met your brother at our town dances, and I even had one pleasure of playing with him on stage at one of our local barn dances."

"Sure, I welcome you to Buffalo, Katie Charlton from Sligo." John extended his hand and officially greeted her. "If you are willing to wait a wee bit, I will be happy to escort you to your new home."

Katie had bewitched John with her smile. She placed her hand in her pocket and rubbed Marion's lucky stone. "Finally, after all our time away, Marion's lucky stone is working its magic."

"Is everything alright, Katie? You seemed so very far away for a moment and I dinna' know what you were thinking?"

"Well, John, I hear a wee bit of an Irish brogue sneaking into your speech." Katie laughed.

"I do work very hard to keep my brogue hidden. Some places in the city do not like the Irish and will not give us jobs. It makes it a little easier if I try to blend in more. Now, I must turn in me gun and sign off for the night. I will be back in just a moment.

Katie sat down on one of the wooden benches in the precinct house and began to reflect on her day.

"How could I be so lucky to stop John Conlon of Tobercurry for help. He is a very handsome man and very young compared to his brother, Paddy. I am sure me Mum and Da are directing my feet in tah right direction from high up in heaven!"

Suddenly, Katie realized that John was standing next to her. "Sorry, John! I was talking to me Mum and Da up in heaven. I am sure both had something to do with me meeting you."

John bent down and picked up Katie's suitcase. Then, he placed his other hand under her elbow and helped her to rise from the bench.

Katie was deeply impressed by John being such a gentleman.

They walked in silence until they reached the trolley stop. "When I first came to Buffalo, I was a conductor on this trolley." John explained. "As soon as I could, I took the Buffalo Police exam and became an officer with the mounted division. I had so much experience with horses back in Ireland on our farm, that this was the perfect position for me. Today, however, was my first day walking the beat. One of the officers became ill, and the Captain asked me if I would take over for him. Otherwise, I would not have been here to meet you."

Once again, Katie put her hand in her pocket and rubbed Marion's magic stone. Then, she whispered a prayer of thanks to all those watching over her from above.

Together they rode the street car and talked comfortably about their adventures since leaving Ireland. John was so impressed with Katie's bravery as she told about leaving home alone onboard ship, and then making her way to the US from Canada.

Time passed quickly, and soon John stood and indicated to the driver that this was their stop. Katie was so happy that she bounded up the aisle and down the stairs.

"Be careful, Katie!" John warned. "I would like to deliver you in one piece!"

Katie laughed. "I am so excited, John! Today is a day filled with first times for me – my first bus ride into a new country, my first trolley ride, and my first police escort!"

As they walked down the street, Katie was amazed by the large homes that were all so close to each other. They even had paved walkways leading up to the houses. Meanwhile, John was laughing and enjoying all Katie's reactions.

Finally, John stopped in the middle of the walk. "Here you are, Katie. Delivered right to the door of 91 Woodside Avenue. Would you like me to wait and make sure we have the right house?"

Katie was already half-way up the walkway when she looked over her shoulder to answer. "Please, John, if you could ..."

Suddenly, Katie was sprawled on the concrete. Her elbows and knees were bloody, but she did not seem to mind. "I never saw a stairway that led up to a front door before! Back home, you just walk from the dirt into the house."

John knelt down and was busy dabbing the blood from Katie's knees, when the front door of the house flew open and a young woman with a long braid of red hair rushed out.

"Oh Katie! Katie! Sure, I canna' believe you are really here, and with a police escort as well!"

John raised his head and put his bloodied handkerchief into his pocket. "Hello! I am John Conlon ..." He never completed his introduction because Katie interrupted.

"John is Paddy Conlon's younger brother from Tobercurry. He is my knight in shining armor and saved me when I was lost in your city."

Nora wrapped her arms around her dearest friend. "I canna' believe you came all by yourself to America. I have missed you so much, and I thank God you are finally here with us. You bring such joy to me heart!"

By this time, Nora's family were all on the porch wiping tears from their eyes. Katie was moved by their emotional welcome. "I love all of you and I have missed you with all of me heart! We have been apart way too long!"

Mrs. Scanlon invited everyone inside where they could continue their reunion in the privacy of their own home. Just as Katie approached the front stairs, John took her arm and whispered, "Remember to walk up the stairs one at a time to get to the front door."

While still climbing the stairs, Katie heard her name screamed from down the street. Marion, followed by her entire family, was running to greet her beloved friend. In her excitement, Katie once again stumbled on the stair, but John took her arm and held her upright.

Marion sobbed as she embraced her forever friend. "I have missed you so much, me dear, and we have so much to tell, but first, I believe you have some cuts that need to be tended to."

"No time for that, Marion! I just want to sit down and absorb having all of you back in me life. Our long-awaited reunion is finally complete!"

Everyone moved inside the Scanlon home and John was automatically accepted as one of their own. Drinks were served, toasts given, and stories exchanged.

Finally, John stood and addressed the families. "Sure, this is the best time I have had since I left Ireland! I thank you for your hospitality and generous welcome. However, I must work the early morning shift tomorrow and I need to get some sleep. Once again, I thank you for a wonderful evening!"

Katie rushed forward, stood on her toes, and kissed John's cheek. "Now that you have met everyone, you must promise to come again!"

Mrs. Scanlon echoed Katie's sentiments and shook John's hand. "Surely, John, it would be our pleasure to have you join us for Sunday morning Mass at nine o'clock. Then, we come home and cook a huge breakfast and spend all day together until we eat our supper. Do not bring anything with you, we have so much food and drink already planned. Just bring yourself!"

"Thank you, Mrs. Scanlon, I would be pleased to join you. I only live a few blocks from here, so I will arrive before Mass." Then he turned his attention to Katie. "Miss Charlton, would you do me the honor of walking with me to Church?"

Blushing bright pink, Katie smiled and shook her head. "I would truly be honored, John."

After John departed, Nora and Marion pulled Katie aside.

"Katie, what is goin' on with you and John Conlon? Nora quizzed.

"Yes, he just said he wants to walk with you to church on Sunday." Marion added.

Katie reached deep into her pocket and retrieved Marion's lucky stone. "It is due to your lucky stone, Marion! Its magic made everything come true for me. I canna' tell you how happy I am you gave it to me before you left Ireland. I am so pleased to give it back to you now."

Marion shook her head. "No, Katie! I want you to keep it. Me lucky stone has shown its power in your hand, and deserves to stay with you!"

Katie smiled and hugged her friend. There were no words to express her thankfulness to Marion and Nora.

The Exchange Street Bus Terminal did not open until 1919, so that international buses disembarked their passengers at the site under construction for the new Central Terminal. That structure was completed in 1929. This historic landmark, although closed in 1979, is currently under extensive renovation.

Although I was just a young child when I visited the functioning terminal, I vividly remember the huge clock that dominated the foyer. Beautiful marble seemed to be everywhere, from the floors to the walls. And, as all small children, a visit to the bathroom was a must – and what an amazing sight!

Art Deco in design, and 17 stories high, the last train departed in October, 1979. The Buffalo Central Terminal was placed on the State and National Registers of Historic Places in 1984.

Once Katie reunited with her friends, she had no intention of returning to Canada. She was Irish, and never planned on becoming a Canadian citizen. Until the day she died at 88 years of age, she remained an illegal alien, and proudly proclaimed her Irish birthright.

My Grandfather, John Conlon, served in the US Infantry during World War I. In return, he was awarded American citizenship. He and my Grandmother were able to return to Ireland using my Grandfather's passport, where my mother, Mary, lived until she was two years old. I still have that passport picture of all three of them framed in my home.

After my Grandfather died in 1955, my Grandmother could no longer travel outside of the country. She never seemed to mind being denied the opportunity to leave the US, because she forever carried Ireland in her heart.

CHAPTER TWENTY-FOUR
♥

Once Katie had settled into her new life, she began work as the downstairs maid in the Gratwick Estate. She enjoyed her work and was always laughing and smiling at everyone she came into contact with. The household loved her, and she was readily accepted as a welcomed addition to the staff.

One Monday morning, Katie arrived at the estate very pale and her eyes were red from crying. The upstairs maid found her in the servant's quarters. Katie was shaking all over and couldn't seem to answer the maid's questions, so she ran to fetch Mrs. Gratwick.

When the lady of the house arrived, Katie was sitting on the cold stone floor with swollen eyes and flushed cheeks. "Katie, whatever has happened? Are you hurt, my dear?"

"I should never have left Ireland, Mam, and now I am about to die."

"Why do you think you are dying, Katie?

"I am bleeding bright red blood for no reason. I dinna' hurt myself, but I am sure to die!"

Mrs. Gratwick looked at Katie's uniform hanging up to dry, and immediately knew what had happened to the young girl.

"Katie, I know that you are nineteen years old, but didn't anyone ever talk to you about the facts of life?"

"The facts of life, Mam? What could life have to do with me death?"

"You are not dying, dear girl. You are becoming a woman. You are a little older than most girls, but I will explain everything to you. Let's get you into one of my robes, and then we will sit in the solarium, have some hot tea and a talk."

After explaining to Katie about womanhood, Mrs. Gratwick felt a special connection to the young girl. She realized that the Irish lass was all alone in a new country without a mother to confide in and help her adjust to a new life. She kissed Katie on the forehead and told her that her chauffeur would drive her home so she could relax for the rest of the day.

After more than a year of employment, Katie had earned the reputation as the most trustworthy employee of the estate. One sunny morning, Mrs. Gratwick was inspecting the living room and became aware of the cobwebs, spiderwebs, and dust gathered along the top of the high ceilings and above the floor-to-ceiling windows. She called Katie into the room. "I must go out this afternoon, Katie, but while I am gone, please pull down all the *Irish curtains* and burn them."

Katie was very confused about Mrs. Gratwick's request. "Are you sure, Mam?" She asked in disbelief.

"Of course I am sure, Katie! There is a step-ladder in the butler's pantry that will make it easier for you to reach. I will be home before supper."

Katie looked up at the beautiful draperies that hung from the high windows. "Maybe this is how rich people change their curtains." She thought aloud.

Katie carried the ladder into the room and began the laborious task of taking down the dark, heavy drapes from all the windows. When that task was completed, she fed the heavy panels into the fireplace. After she had disposed of all the ashes, Katie cleaned the windows, inside and out. The room looked so bright and cheerful that Katie no longer questioned Mrs. Gratwick's strange request.

As promised, Mrs. Gratwick returned home before five o'clock. She strolled into the living room and couldn't quite figure out why the room looked so dazzlingly bright and inviting. Then, it struck her ... the custom-made drapes were gone!

"Katie!" She called out. "Please come into the living room."

Katie rushed into the room. "Yes, Mam."

"Where are my velvet draperies?"

"Sure, you told me to take down the Irish curtains and burn them, Mam." Katie whispered. "Did I do something wrong?"

Mrs. Gratwick thought for a few minutes and then began to laugh. Katie still had no idea what she had done to make Mrs. Gratwick react in this peculiar manner.

Well, Katie," she began, "it looks like you will be using your talents as a master lace maker to make new curtains for all these windows. I must say, the sunlight is a very pleasant addition to this normally dark room."

"I dunna' know what I did wrong," Katie apologized, "but I am truly sorry. I will be happy to make lace curtains in my spare time."

"Oh, Katie, you are precious! The term *Irish curtains* refers to the cobwebs and dust that has gathered high up on the ceiling, not the actual drapes!" Mrs. Gratwick explained.

"Oh, no!" Katie sobbed. "Will I lose me job now, Mam?"

"No, my dear, you will keep your job. It is actually my fault for not explaining the task so that you completely understood what I wanted you to do. I am sure that my husband and I will have a great laugh about this over our evening meal!"

Katie began to back from the room. "One minute, Katie." Mrs. Gratwick stopped her. "I understand from the other maids that you send all of your money home to Ireland and leave nothing for yourself. Is that true, my dear?"

"Not exactly, Mam." Katie began to explain. "I just keep out enough money for me bus fare to and from work, plus I give a wee bit to Mrs. Scanlon for letting me sleep at her house on my days off from work."

"Oh, my dear generous girl! You must keep some of your money for your own expenses and enjoyment. When you decided to leave Ireland, your sister never intended for you to send almost your entire paycheck to her. Your friends here are very concerned. They say that you never go out with them because you do not have any money. Not even ten cents for the moving pictures, Katie?"

Katie lowered her head. She was terribly embarrassed that Mrs. Gratwick was disappointed in her.

"I am so sorry, Mam! I dunna' understand all the costs here in America, so I thought I was doin' right for Eliza and Liam."

Mrs. Gratwick reached out and took Katie's hand. "I will help you, my dear. We will set up a budget for you, and then you will see how much money you have left to send to your sister. Eliza would never expect you to do without personal things that you need. Is there something that you would like to buy right now?"

Katie breathed a sigh of relief. "New shoes would be wonderful, Mam! These belonged to Eliza and are very tight on me feet. I have been tending all my blisters as best as I can after I finish my day's chores."

"Well then, tomorrow we will drive into town and you will purchase a new pair of shoes." Mrs. Gratwick smiled. "Now, off with you and eat your supper. Let the rest of your work go until after we shop for your new shoes tomorrow!"

Katie was so happy that she hummed a happy tune on her way to the kitchen. She loved her job, and Mrs. Gratwick treated her like family. The only thing missing from her life was Eliza and Liam.

The burning of the *Irish curtains* is another true story from my Grandmother's life. She had so much to learn about not taking every word literally. American humor, sarcasm, and irony were all very difficult for her to understand. It took years for her to appreciate their meanings!

Additionally, my Grandmother did send all her money home to Eliza and Liam in Ireland. When Mrs. Gratwick was informed by the other maids, she took Katie aside and taught her how to budget so that she had money of her own to spend.

Although not eligible for Social Security in her older years, and having only my Grandfather's small pension from the Police Department, she was always generous to a fault. Grandmother always gave us money for Birthdays, Easter, Christmas, and any other special occasion. After she passed away, I found an envelope with my name written on the front. Inside was a hand-written card welcoming our new baby into the world. Folded tightly inside, was a ten-dollar bill. Catherine was born eight weeks later, and named for her Great-Grandmother.

It was also true that my Grandmother did not know the facts of life when she arrived in the US. Eliza always thought of her as the baby of the family, and since Katie was small in stature, and sickly most of her younger years, Eliza did not feel the need to prepare her for womanhood. At nineteen years of age, Mrs. Gratwick educated her favorite downstairs maid in all that she would need to know in life!

CHAPTER TWENTY-FIVE

♥

As the months passed, John Conlon began a formal courtship with Katie Charlton. Unfortunately, planning the wedding was a wee bit difficult, since Katie was only home in South Buffalo on weekends. Also, Katie was determined to continue working for the Gratwick family until her wedding.

Every Saturday night, Nora, Marion, Katie, and John, would walk a few blocks to the home of Nellie and Mike Murray. They were a newly married couple from Ireland, who loved to host dances in their home.

At the start of the evening, the men would move all the furniture to one side of the room, and then proceed to roll up the rug so that the hardwood floor was exposed. As soon as the guest musician arrived, the dancing began. Jigs and reels filled the air as the sound of hard-heeled shoes traced intricate dance patterns around the room.

The Murray house would literally rock from all the noise, but no one in the neighborhood ever complained … the south side of Buffalo was settled by the Irish, and they all enjoyed a good dancing party!

It was at one of these gatherings, Marion McGlone met one of the new neighbors, John

Donohue. Marion was a wonderful dancer, light on her feet and very graceful despite her larger size. John had been watching her for several weeks, until he garnered enough courage to ask her to be his partner. They were a striking couple, and immediately became inseparable.

Nora, on the other hand, danced with everyone. Her distinctive laughter filled the room as she whirled around with her various partners. Nora had no desire to begin a romantic relationship. Her life was full and she was very happy. During the week, Nora worked at the Abbott Estate. She was treated as a member of their family and spoiled the two small children in the home. Extremely physically fit, Nora walked everywhere. She always walked at a brisk pace, her arms swinging with each step.

When the Saturday night dance was half-over, the musicians took their break, and the women delivered their food to the dining room table. A large punchbowl was set in the middle of the table for the women, while the men imbibed in a 'wee drink' from their flasks.

After the break, the second-half of the night consisted of guests manning their own instruments to entertain the crowd. Penny whistles, bodhrans, fiddles, and even a bagpipe, would take center stage for the sing-along portion of the evening.

As always, the last song of the evening was *The Parting Glass*, as the guests raised their glasses and toasted.

When the evening ended, once again, Marion, Nora, Katie, and John would head for home. Now, however, a new individual was added to their group – John Donohue.

Nora, like all her friends from Sligo, was a terrible cook. Everything that she made was boiled ... not just boiled, but boiled in the cabbage water that was always on the stovetop.

Nora did have one very strange habit. She would cool some of the cabbage water in a glass pitcher and place it in the icebox. The entire kitchen always smelled like cabbage. However, every morning, Nora would drink a glass of cold cabbage water before she took her brisk walk!

When Nora was well into her 80's, she had a terrible fall and broke her hip. The Abbotts insisted that she convalesce at the estate so that they could take care of her themselves. They were a wonderful family and cared for her until she passed.

Lastly, Marion McGlone married John Donohue and they bought a home in South Buffalo to raise their family.

As an aside, when I visited my Great Uncle Paddy Conlon in Tobercurry, Ireland, he was very proud when he announced that he had procured bacon for my breakfast. He smiled when he told me that everyone knew how *Yanks* loved their bacon. Imagine my surprise when I discovered that he had boiled the bacon in the cabbage water left from supper the night before!

On my Grandmother's 86th Birthday, she asked me to hold her hand so that she could stand up and dance an Irish jig. Perhaps it was the celebratory Irish whiskey she drank, or perhaps it was an item from her bucket list, but she danced! Clicking her heels together, she laughed and laughed.

CHAPTER TWENTY-SIX

♥

John Conlon became engaged to Catherine Charlton in January 1920. The bands were to be announced in the Church of The Holy Family in South Buffalo, and the wedding vows exchanged in April of that year.

The groom had all his papers in order from when he entered The United States through Ellis Island, and also served in the US Army. Katie, however, did not have any official papers, and sent to Kilmacowen Parish for the Church records.

In March, 1920, an anxiously awaited package arrived from Kilmacowen. Katie ripped open the envelope and spread the various documents across the dining room table.

"A mistake! It must be a mistake!" Katie cried. "Surely, it must be a mistake! It must be a wrong Catherine Charlton!"

Nora and Marion rushed to the dining room to check on their friend. "Katie!" Nora called. "Whatever has happened? Why in heaven's name are you so upset?"

Katie pointed down at the table and indicated all the papers strewn haphazardly across one of her tablecloths. Marion picked up the document that was closest to her, sat down and began to read.

"Oh my, Katie! I can see why you are so upset." She then handed the birth certificate to Nora.

Nora took her time perusing the document before she spoke. "I dunna' see any problem here. Am I missing something?"

Marion was quickly losing patience with her cousin. "Look at the date, Nora! Read carefully and pay attention to all dates on each of Katie's official documents."

Nora began reading aloud. "Catherine Charlton, daughter of Anne Monaghan Charlton and John Charlton. Sure, 'tis true. Born on eighteenth day of February in 1889."

Katie gasped! "Me birth date canna' be correct. We must carefully examine each one of these documents and check to see where the mistake was first made."

The three girls sat down at the table carefully reading each sheet of the many documents. The result was always the same ... Katie was born on February 18, 1889 and not March 17, 1891."

Katie put her head down on the table and sobbed. Nora looked at Marion in total confusion. She couldn't understand why her dear friend was in so much pain. Marion quietly whispered in her ear. "Katie always thought her birthday was on the feast of Saint Patrick, and now she knows 'tis not true."

Nora interrupted Marion with one of her obvious questions. "So, what does one month difference make to Katie? March or February, is it really significant?"

Marion sighed. "Nora, 'tis not the month that Katie is upset over, 'tis the year. All her records state she was born in 1889."

Nora giggled. "1889 was a good year, Marion! Both of us were born in 1889!"

Katie raised her head from the table. "John, me beloved fiancé, was born December second in 1891. Bejabbers! I am two years older!"

Marion, always the common-sense one of the three, consoled Katie. "We will give all the paperwork to Father Rafferty when we go to confession. He will never be able to tell another living soul since he is bound by the secrecy of the confessional."

Katie looked into her friend's bright blue eyes. "Yes, Marion, Father Rafferty canna' tell anyone what he is told in his confession box! You are so smart to remember something so important from our religion classes! You, me dearest, have made me happy again!"

The three girls hugged each other while Katie kissed their cheeks.

"How I love both of you for helping me solve one of me most devasting problems in me life!"

The year of my Grandmother's birth was indeed another obstacle for her to overcome once she was settled in America.

Historically, Irish men did not marry until they were well into their thirties. Then, they always married younger women. Katie thought that she would be ostracized by her friends and neighbors once they discovered that John Conlon was about to marry an *older* woman! Katie was determined to keep her actual age a secret from everyone – including her future husband!

Years later, when my Grandfather passed, my Grandmother had her name, date, and year of birth engraved on the tombstone along with my Grandfather's information. Just one problem … she purposely had the wrong year of birth placed on her side of the monument – namely, 1891.

My Father, the son-in-law, always teased my Grandmother about her knocking two years off her real age. He would joke that if she misbehaved, he was going to the cemetery and chisel the correct year into the headstone. Every time my Dad said this, we would all laugh at my Grandmother's horrified reaction.

CHAPTER TWENTY-SEVEN
♥

John hurried from the trolley and down the street toward the Scanlon home. He carried travel brochures and all the paperwork necessary for the issuance of a passport.

John was excited – he had decided that Ireland was the perfect spot for Katie and his wedding trip. Since Eliza and Liam could not leave the farm and travel to The United States, John would take his precious bride to them instead. He smiled as he thought that this trip would be the perfect *icing on the wedding cake*!

Meanwhile, John had secretly contacted Patrick O'Hara, the bursar from Katie's ship that sailed from Ireland, and Patrick was happy to accept John's invitation to the wedding. The same was true for Katie's shipboard friend, Anna Ford, who was also coming to Buffalo from Rochester. John was so happy when he thought of their reunion. Everything was now going forward exactly as he had planned.

Katie was sitting on the front porch when she spotted John rushing down the street. "And, me darlin', what bee is stinging your bottom to make you go so fast?" Katie laughed.

John smiled up at the love of his life. "I have such wonderful news to share with you! I just had to rush home and tell you!"

Katie stumbled as she ran down the stairs to greet her intended. John, as always, was right there to catch her. Katie looked up into his deep blue eyes and saw all her love reflected right back at her.

"How did I ever survive me clumsiness growing up in Ireland without you to rescue me?" Katie didn't wait for John's answer as she planted a kiss on his cheek. "I will never get used to houses having all these stairs just to get to the front door!" She giggled.

It was then that Katie noticed the papers that John was holding in his hand. "Sure, what do you have here?"

As Katie read, her face lost all color and tears began to well up behind her eyes. "Ireland, John? You want to go home to Ireland?"

"It is a surprise, my love! My wedding gift to you!" John happily explained. "We can share the fact that we are husband and wife with Eliza and Liam."

Katie took John's hand and silently led him into the house. "Please sit down, John. I am afraid I have some news I need to share with you, but I just dunna' know where to begin."

John gave Katie's hand a reassuring squeeze and pulled her down next to him on the couch. "Start at the beginning, my love, and please tell me what it is that is troubling you."

"John," Katie began with a trembling voice, "I canna' ever return to Ireland because I will surely be arrested by British Police. I am a fugitive - a friend of a rebel, James Connolly, who was executed for his part in our Easter Uprising of 1916. After it failed, English soldiers scoured our countryside arresting anyone who had a relationship with any rebels. Eliza and Liam put me on a ship bound for America in order to keep me safe."

"Oh Katie, that was four years ago. You surely cannot believe that they would still be searching for you?"

"No, John, 'tis so much more serious!" Katie continued. "I left Ireland so quickly we dinna' have any time to get proper paperwork to enter at Ellis Island. I was sent to Toronto, Canada, where I was issued temporary papers stamped *political asylum*."

"I know all this, Katie. That is how you met Patrick and Anna. I really do remember all the details that you told me."

"No, John, I dinna' tell you all me details." Katie tried to explain in a coherent manner. "When I left Canada, I dinna' have permission to enter and stay here permanently. I only had temporary papers good for ten days, and I was supposed to appear before the magistrate for my permanent papers. I never went back, John! I was so afraid, I just couldna' go back. So, I pretended I was legal, when in fact, I am still illegal!"

John sat in silence while he digested all that Katie had revealed. "Did you ever intend on becoming a US citizen?"

"I am Irish, John, and I never wanted to be anything else but Irish. So, since no one in the government came after me, I was happy to go along with my life as it is today. But now I realize my dream to see Eliza and Liam will never come true. I can never go home again!"

John stood, kissed Katie goodbye, and placed his paperwork on the table before he walked out the door. "I will see what I can do to fix this problem. Please, Katie, do not cry. I would never ask you to give up being Irish. Your love for our homeland is one reason I fell in love with you. As soon as I can, I will let you know what I learn from the Immigration Officials."

Then, John was gone.

Hours passed, and still John had not returned from his mission. Katie began pacing back-and-forth in the living room, while Nora and Marion attempted to read the evening paper.

Finally, Nora and Marion had enough of Katie's nervous energy and suggested that they all take a walk.

"Let's get some fresh air." Nora strongly suggested. "We can walk toward tah trolley stop John uses when he comes for a visit."

Everyone agreed and headed for the door, only stopping long enough to grab their coats. Nora, in the lead, paused on the porch and turned to Katie. "Now, me dear friend, remember we have stairs that lead down to the walkway.

No falling, please! John is not here to catch you this time!"

Suddenly, the tension was broken, and all three were laughing together.

The girls didn't have to travel far before they saw John briskly walking toward them. Marion was the first to speak. "Looks like our John is on a mission! Nora, let us turn around and walk back toward your house. Katie and John will surely need private time for a wee talk."

Katie smiled her thanks at her two treasured friends.

As John advanced, he seemed very happy and smiled at his fiancé. Instantly, Katie knew that John had worked his magic and that everything was going to be alright. She ran toward John and flung herself into his arms.

"You look so happy, John! Is everything going to be settled for us?"

"Of course, my love! I have met with several Immigration Officials, and since I served in the infantry in World War I, I am a citizen and I am eligible for a passport. Since you will be my wife once we marry, you will be allowed to travel under my passport. We must have our picture taken together as soon as possible and file our paperwork. Once we have our marriage license, we can leave for Ireland."

"I was so worried, John!" Katie confided. "I never told anyone about being here illegally. Now, once I marry my knight in shining armor, I will be free to return home. Let us go and start making plans. We have so many loved ones to visit back home. Oh, John, I am so excited! You are my very own hero, and I will love you forever and ever!"

Following World War I, the government of The United States, allowed families to travel together on one passport as long as the person issued the passport was an American citizen.

The photograph on my Grandfather's passport shows my Grandmother, Catherine, my Grandfather, John, and a wide-eyed toddler, Mary Ann (my Mom).

This practice was discontinued when The United States became embroiled in World War II. Then, both the husband and the wife had to prove their citizenship.

CHAPTER TWENTY-EIGHT

♥

Katie and John were married in April 1920.

The happy couple returned to Ireland for an extended visit. They lived in Sligo until my Mother, their firstborn, was almost two years old.

Mary's birth was followed by the birth of their son, John. Unfortunately, he passed away at age four due to a ruptured appendix. A second son, died in infancy.

Despite the tragedies in their lives, John and Katie were very happy. When their daughter Mary married Patrick Morrisey, they said *we do too*, and lived with us for the rest of their lives.

In the early years of their marriage, John Conlon sponsored many relatives from Ireland and Scotland who wished to come to The United States. James Charlton, Katie's devoted brother, was one of the first. He lived with my Grandparents until he had earned enough money to bring his wife, Mary Jane, and his children over from Scotland. Finally, Katie and James were reunited!

My Grandfather, John, passed away in June, 1955, leaving behind his grieving wife, daughter, and four Grandchildren. 'Poppy' was waked in our living room, and as a small child, I could not understand why he didn't answer me when I climbed up on the kneeler and whispered in his ear. How I loved this big, happy man who always had a piece of candy hidden in his shirt pocket for me!

My Grandmother, Katie, passed away in March 1977. She lived a long life surrounded by her growing family of Grandchildren and Great-Grandchildren. One of her greatest joys was talking about Ireland. Although she out-lived both Nora and Marion, they continued to live through her wonderful stories.

When I attended College in Ireland, I was able to visit all of our relatives. I walked in Yeats Woods, stood in the shadow of Ben Bulben, and walked on the railroad tracks where the Charlton cottage had once stood for generations.

As a youngster, my Dad would take us to Crystal Beach, an amusement park just over the Peace Bridge in Canada. One year, my Dad decided to bring my Grandmother along with us for the day. We all worked with her so that she would be able to answer the Immigration Officer with one word – Buffalo – when asked where she was born.

We were all excited about a day at the park and the opportunity to ride the old wooden roller coaster called the *Comet*. We jabbered on about the bumper cars, the Magic Carpet, and most of all, the assortment of foods available to us.

Sometimes, the best laid plans, go astray – and that was exactly what happened to all of us. When we entered the Canadian Immigration Plaza, the inspector stuck his head into the car window and asked everyone where they were born. We all held our breath as we heard Grandmother proudly proclaim, '*Sligo, Ireland*!'

Dad just turned the car around and headed back home. We could not enter Canada without my Grandmother's *'non-existent'* paperwork!

The ride home was completely silent. We were all sad to have missed the opportunity to spend a day at the amusement park. However, it was impossible to stay perturbed with my Grandmother. Her Irish wit, the sparkle in her eyes, and her love of family always carried her through every situation in her life.

Katie was Irish! She even refused the government's proposal of amnesty for illegals living in The United States.

Katie Charlton Conlon died proud of the fact that she carried Ireland forever, deep in her heart until the very end.

THE END

ACKNOWLEDGEMENTS

♥

There are so many individuals that I wish to thank for encouraging me in my quest to write this work of Historical Fiction.

First, my family, both here and abroad, especially my Maternal Grandparents who shared so much of their lives with me.

Second, the late Sister Patricia Smith, GNSH, who instilled in me my love for history while I studied at D'Youville College in Buffalo, New York. I can still recall all the dates from significant events in history … forever committed to my memory.

A tip of the hat to Mr. David Lamb, my Irish Literature Professor at D'Youville. David shared his love for Irish Lit and also recommended me as a candidate for the Irish Scholarship Program.

Special thanks to The University College Dublin, Ireland, and their many visiting Professors. All our historical field trips, as well as the copious notes I wrote during my classes, were all utilized in this manuscript. This adventure was a true highlight in my education.

Lastly, my gratitude to the late Sister Sylvia, SSJ, my high school English teacher at Victory Academy in Lackawanna, New York. Sister taught me to believe in my ability to write and encouraged me to always dream big!

ABOUT THE AUTHOR
♥

Kate is a retired high school and college English teacher with a love of family, the English language, and history.

First published in her senior year of high school by St. Bonaventure Press, Kate also was a contributor to her college newspaper. Additionally, four of her educational articles have been published by Hyperion Press (Disney).

In her spare time, Kate is an avid reader who voraciously devours non-fiction and historical works of fiction.

Never allowing herself to have idle hands, Kate, like her Grandmother, does all forms of needlework – from knitting to counted cross stitch. The only difference is that the *'south paw'* has taught herself to craft using her right hand!

Kate's best friend is her husband of 43 years, Steve. They are proud parents of two grown daughters, two Grandchildren, four fur-grand-pets and her own Golden Retriever, Ms. Morgan.

AN IRISH LANGUAGE PRIMER

♥

The Irish language has three main dialects, Connacht, Munster, and Ulster. All students must study Gaelic as a second language; however, teachers always utilize a standardized combination of these three dialects.

Vowels:
a as in the word '*bat*'
í as in the '*fee*'
á as in the sound '*aw*'

o as in the word '*son*'
e as in the word '*pet*'
ó as in the word '*glow*'
é as in the word '*grey*'
u as in the word '*took*'
i as in the word '*hit*'
ú as in the word '*rule*'

Consonants:

The Irish language uses what English speakers feel is a mismatched combination of consonants that together make their own sound.

bh is pronounced as the letter '*v*'
bhf is pronounced as a '*w*'
c is pronounced as a '*k*'

Consonants: (continued)

ch is pronounced like the guttural *German sound ch*

d is pronounced like our letter '*d*' when it is followed by a *broad vowel*, and **d** is pronounced as the letter '*j*' when followed by a *slender vowel*.

Remember, *slender vowels* are **i** and **e**, while the *broad vowels* are **a**, **e**, **o**, and **u**.

Made in the
USA
Middletown, DE